The Ledger of Worlds

By Ilir Nina

The Ledger of Worlds

The Ledger of Worlds, Volume 1

Ilir Nina

Published by Ilir Nina, 2026.

Ledger of the Worlds

By Ilir Nina

Copyright

THE LEDGER OF WORLDS

First edition. January 18, 2026.

ISBN: 979-8992526387

Written by Ilir Nina.

Also by Ilir Nina

my flight to freedom series
Echoes of the Mind
The Final Audit
My flight to freedom II: Shadows and Light: Survival and the American Dream

The Ledger of Worlds
The Ledger of Worlds

Standalone
My Flight to Freedom

Watch for more at https://ilirninaauthor.com/.

Table of Contents

"Every life leaves a mark. Every choice leaves a trail. Somewhere beyond time, the ledger remembers them all."

— Ilir Nina

CHAPTER ONE:

THE SILENCE OF THE BUREAU

The station hung in the cradle of space like an ornament suspended in eternity. It orbited the planet Virellen, a sapphire world veined with silver oceans and crystalline mountain chains that caught distant starlight and fractured it into shimmering beams. Seen from orbit, the planet resembled a living gem, swirling with luminous cloud formations that rippled like silk caught in a cosmic wind. Its cities, designed in concentric spirals, emitted a steady pulse of soft luminescence that traveled upward and reflected across the dark void. Each settlement formed intricate geometric patterns, as though humanity had tried to etch meaning into the surface of a world that refused to answer.

Above, the void did not stretch into emptiness. It pulsed with presence. Dust clouds the size of continents drifted in shades of violet, gold, and iridescent blue. They curled around one another in silent unending dance. The Helion Arm of the galaxy arched far beyond sight, a river of stars that wove through darkness like a celestial spine. The light of those distant suns seemed to move slowly, as though reluctant to abandon the space between them. Within that river lived civilizations older than humanity's myths, each one bound by a cosmic architecture of laws and obligations that humans barely understood.

Here, navigation corridors looped around the station like strands of living light. Thin, luminous conduits stretched outward in gentle curves, guiding vessels along fixed gravitational currents. Freighter ships glided through these pathways without making a sound. Their hulls held no visible engines, but the air around them rippled faintly from the energy fields they emitted. Each vessel transported more than goods. Some carried fragments of culture, encoded philosophies, genetic archives, or ideas refined into tangible exchanges. Others moved intangible resources: belief tax credits, emotional resonance licenses, memory bonds, and consciousness transfers.

To an untrained observer, these trades would have seemed impossible to quantify. Yet in this region of the Helion Arm, ideas were as valuable as ore, and identity was a recognized commodity.

Automated drones zipped across docking rings, weaving through the arriving and departing ships. Their paths left trails of ion mist that curled and dispersed like smoke in cold air. They scanned vessel hulls, verified trade invoices, and collected declarations of intent, which were considered more important than the cargo itself. Intent was currency. Motive was risk. Desire was liability.

At the center of this elaborate orbital dance stood Helios Spire, the station that housed the most powerful institution humanity had ever constructed. The Spire rose from a circular core and expanded outward in spiraling layers, each one shaped like a metallic petal. These petals glowed softly, reflecting cosmic radiation and converting it into energy that coursed along the station's surfaces in shimmering veins. Viewed from afar, the station resembled a lotus blooming in space, untouched by time or erosion. It radiated calm, beauty, and control.

Helios Spire was more than a station. It was a declaration.

Here, space was not empty. It breathed. It shimmered. It waited.

And within its immaculate corridors resided the institution responsible for deciding the fate of civilizations.

The Interplanetary Trade and Ethics Bureau.

Its exterior did not threaten. Its surfaces were clean, smooth, and precisely measured. Towers curved upward with angles so perfect that architects debated whether the structure represented mathematics or worship. Transparent windows caught ambient starlight and held it, diffusing illumination gently across the halls. Nothing about the design shouted dominance, yet dominance permeated every inch of it.

The Bureau did not need to appear menacing. It did not enforce order with force. It enforced order by defining the very fabric of existence.

It watched human intention. It weighed purpose. It tracked meaning.

Inside those walls, the universe was not interpreted. It was measured.

Inside those walls, silence was not absence. It was authority.

THE SILENCE INSIDE

Ardent Voss hated silence.

It was not the silence of solitude or the quiet of early morning reflection. It was a silence that pressed inward. The walls of the Bureau absorbed sound with unsettling efficiency, swallowing footsteps and dampening speech until every noise seemed like an intrusion. Even breathing felt monitored, as though the building preferred auditors who did not need air.

Consciousness stabilizers were embedded in the walls. They balanced emotional activity, flattening sudden impulses and softening instinct. Passion, curiosity, excitement, fear, and ambition faded the moment they appeared. The Bureau did not outlaw emotion. It neutralized it.

Silence here was a weapon.

Ardent's office resembled containment more than workspace. Pale graphite walls absorbed light, turning every reflection into fog. Metallic floors radiated a subtle chill beneath his shoes. A single narrow window overlooked Virellen, but Bureau filters washed out the planet's natural beauty, muting its blues into gray and dissolving any hint of warmth. Nothing outside looked alive.

His desk was made of obsidian polymer, polished to a mirror finish. On it sat three curved monitors that formed a half circle of luminescent white. They streamed lines of information at speeds that would fracture an untrained mind. Trade codes, compliance measures, psychological indexes, motive hierarchies, and purpose vectors scrolled relentlessly. Their glow hardened Ardent's expression, as if the screens sculpted the contours of his face into sharp angles.

A notification pulsed in the lower corner of his central display.

Discrepancy Detected

Ardent leaned closer. The words blinked, pale and insistent. It was the fifth time this week. He exhaled, fogging the corner of his left lens before the moisture dissipated.

He was in his mid thirties, though most assumed he was older. His hair refused to stay neat, falling in uneven strands across his forehead. His eyes were a pale storm gray, always focused past what was visible, searching the gap between data points where truth tended to hide. His clothing was compliant and unremarkable. His posture carried a permanent forward lean, as if the universe was slightly ahead of him and he could never quite catch it.

Ardent did not fear complexity. He feared unresolved questions.

His parents had raised him in a settlement where precision was worshiped more fervently than any deity. They were compliance engineers who insisted that civilization survived only when rules held firm. Emotion was classified as a disruptive force. Feelings were indulgences. Questions were measured for necessity.

Ardent learned to categorize thought before understanding feeling. He entered the Bureau while others his age still debated what they wanted from life. He never sought promotion. The Bureau raised him because he solved what others could not. His mind did not avoid knots. It untied them.

He stared at the blinking notification.

"Again," he muttered.

THE SUPERVISOR ARRIVES

A voice cut through the heavy quiet.

"You are obsessing again."

Ardent did not turn. He recognized the tone before the words had fully reached him.

Seren Hale stood in the doorway. She was in her forties, but the contours of her face suggested a timelessness that resisted age. Her uniform was immaculate, formed without wrinkle or error. Her presence was not loud, yet no one ignored it. She moved with the certainty of someone who never questioned her place in the world.

Authority did not cling to her. It radiated from her.

"Obsession is necessary here," Ardent replied.

"Only until it blinds the observer," Seren answered. "There is a point where diligence ceases to serve truth and begins to shape it."

Ardent looked up at her. "Is that an accusation?"

"It is recognition."

He turned back to his monitors and summoned the anomaly. Endless rows of planetary compliance entries materialized. Each row represented a transaction humanity had made with the Exchange. Some were material trades. Others involved transfers of cultural rights, symbolic assets, or intellectual patterns. A few were harder to categorize, structured around philosophical obligations or existential commitments.

Something was missing.

Entire epochs had been erased.

"These records are not incomplete," Ardent said. "They were dismantled and reconstructed."

Seren was silent.

Ardent understood this silence.

Not hesitation.

Warning.

"What debt does humanity owe that someone believes we are safer forgetting we ever incurred it?" he asked.

Seren's jaw tightened. "Curiosity does not grant clearance."

"Protocols do not bury history."

She hesitated. Her voice softened, almost imperceptibly. "Truth is often more costly than belief."

She walked away, leaving Ardent with the silence he hated most.

The silence that follows revelation.

THE LEDGER AND THE LIE

Ardent accessed an old archival node, bypassing revoked permissions. The system resisted, then yielded. Fragments of encrypted data assembled into a lattice of symbols.

A hidden ledger emerged.

ACQUISITION: SENTIENT BASELINE CONSCIOUSNESS

COLLATERAL: HUMAN COGNITIVE POTENTIAL

Humanity had borrowed intelligence.

ACQUISITION: CULTURAL ENLIGHTENMENT ACCELERATION

COLLATERAL: MEMORY OF ORIGIN

Humanity had traded its past.

Then the entry that chilled him:

REPAYMENT FAILURE NOTICE

STATUS: PENDING CORRECTION

DATE: 1,976 YEARS AGO

Humans had forgotten their debt.

But the universe had not.

His wrist console vibrated. A message appeared:

Stop. You cannot pay the cost.

We tried once. Never again.

Ardent typed:

"Who are you?"

The reply:

The Forgotten

Silence returned.

Not empty.

Predatory.

THE BUREAU EXPOSED

Seren Hale presided over the disciplinary hearing. Three officials sat behind her. Their expressions were carved from neutrality.

"You violated clearance," Seren said.

"You erased history," Ardent replied. "Humanity is collateral on a loan we did not know we took."

"Understanding the debt is not required for survival," Seren answered. "Ignorance protects us."

Ignorance was not flaw.

Ignorance was design.

His badge dissolved. Permissions collapsed. Bureau propaganda flickered overhead.

Humanity shapes its destiny

Ardent whispered:

"No. Humanity rents it."

THE TRUTH HE CANNOT UNSEE

He returned to his apartment, a room as barren and functional as his mind had once been. He accessed the final encrypted document.

PRIMARY ACQUISITION: LICENSE OF ASCENSION

COLLATERAL: HUMAN ESSENCE

TERMS: REPAYMENT UPON MORAL MATURITY

STATUS: DELINQUENT

AUDIT TRIGGER: 7 CYCLES

Seven years remained.

Then a final entry appeared.

We passed once. The cost was unbearable.

Ardent spoke into the quiet.

"What cost?"

The silence did not answer.

It waited.

It listened.

It felt alive.

CHAPTER TWO

THE HIDDEN COLUMNS

Ardent Voss woke to numbers.

They did not appear as digits or symbols, not at first. They came as shapes, rising from some internal horizon of dreams. Towers made of calculation. Columns built from patterns, their foundations glowing faintly, as if holding ancient meaning. Some columns appeared whole. Others bore perfect wounds, missing pieces near their base, the absence pulsing like a living thing. The gaps did not weaken the structures. They defined them.

Ardent hovered in the space between sleep and waking, caught in the silent logic of the dream, until awareness tugged him back into his body.

The white filtered light of his apartment seeped into his vision. He inhaled slowly, allowing the images to settle.

The numbers had spoken to him. Not with words, but through grammar older than language. He saw now what the dream had been showing him. The missing elements were not destruction. They were design.

Someone had rearranged history to hide the truth.

He whispered into the still air:

"They carved the absence."

His voice sounded foreign. Not because of the words, but because of the confidence beneath them. Confidence was not a sanctioned emotion within the Bureau.

He rose, the cold metal floor anchoring him. There was nothing indulgent in his living space. No artifacts. No comforts. Nothing personal. Bureau doctrine taught that identity was distraction. Ardent had accepted that once. Now he wondered if the absence of identity had been purchased.

A SYSTEM THAT PRETENDED TO BE WHOLE

He brewed tea. Bitter. Black. Functional.

The warmth steadied his hands. He activated his home terminal and linked the encrypted drive. The holographic display rose slowly, like a memory returning despite protest.

PRIMARY ACQUISITION: LICENSE OF ASCENSION

COLLATERAL: HUMAN ESSENCE

He tasted the words as if they were poison.

Humanity had mortgaged itself. Not its resources. Not its future.

Its essence.

He felt a cold pressure in his lungs. Fear threatened to bloom but he extinguished it. Emotion clouded clarity. He needed clarity.

The ledger fragment from yesterday glowed in the room. He queried surrounding entries. The familiar reply appeared.

No additional records found

That was the lie.

He opened comparison charts. He examined degradation signatures. He cross referenced entropy models from civilizations whose ledgers had collapsed naturally over millennia.

None matched.

Entropy left fingerprints. This ledger had none.

Natural decay was messy. This silence was immaculate.

Someone had polished the lie.

He layered the gaps across time. First the voids fell randomly. Then subtle rhythms emerged. They aligned with regularly scheduled moral evaluations. They pulsed when repayment cycles should have occurred.

The blank spaces were not damage.

They were intention.

Ardent leaned closer. He whispered:

"Who taught us to forget?"

The question tasted forbidden. It ignited something in his chest. A sense of trespass. A sense of awakening.

He told himself the next step was procedure, not obsession.

He lied.

THE SHADOW COLUMNS

Ardent summoned the forgotten forensic tool.

The utility unfurled without asking permission. Obsolete, overlooked, dismissed by most. But not by him. He had requested access during his first cycle at the Bureau, out of curiosity he never admitted. He now realized he had been preparing for this moment long before he understood why.

The tool did not interpret ledger entries. It interpreted the absence beneath them.

Hex grids appeared. The visible ledger floated in pale light. The erased history manifested as vertical lanes of darkness. These were not random voids. They were structural. They were scars.

He ran his finger along one.

Humanity had been audited many times. Each audit cycle should have asked for repayment. Each repayment should have shaped the next era of humanity. Each era was missing.

The blanks were identical in shape and spacing.

Someone had carved existence into pieces, then removed the moments that defined cost.

Every pillar of human civilization sat upon hollow foundations.

He stared until his eyes blurred.

The dream returned. The wounded towers. The missing base stones. The numbers that held meaning through absence.

Ardent felt his pulse in his throat.

"We were built to forget," he whispered.

HER SHADOW IN HIM

Seren Hale's voice slid into his thoughts unbidden. Her words from yesterday echoed with quiet force.

"Truth is often more costly than belief."

He hated that she had been right.

He hated that he cared she was right.

He had admired Seren for years, though admiration was an unauthorized emotional state. He respected her competence. He envied her certainty. He feared her judgment. He noticed the way she stood, the way silence bent around her, the way her gaze pinned a person without ever lifting her voice.

His reaction to her was not rational.

It was not permitted.

He did not know when it had begun. Perhaps when she first reviewed one of his audits. Or when she placed a hand lightly on his shoulder during a training rotation, telling him that accuracy was a kindness, not an obsession. Her tone then had been calm. Almost warm.

He wondered if she remembered that moment. He wondered if she ever thought of him at all.

Then he hated that the question mattered.

He forced himself back to the ledger. He needed logic, not desire.

Yet desire lingered.

The Bureau taught auditors to sever emotions because emotions created purpose. Purpose created debt. Debt produced consequence.

He now saw the trap inside the teaching.

Purpose was collateral. Humanity had once traded its essence for meaning. The Bureau maintained control by limiting that meaning.

Seren had been taught to enforce the rules.

Ardent had been taught to find the gaps.

He now stood somewhere between.

THE FIRST CUSTODIAN APPEARS

Light thickened in the corner of the room as though illumination itself were being pulled into a vortex. Pixels trembled and rearranged into a shape that flickered between form and suggestion.

Ardent froze.

A Custodian.

Not a being. Not a person. A role. A voice of the Exchange.

"Auditor Ardent Voss," it spoke, calm as an equation. "This reconstruction tool is outside your species tier."

Ardent's mouth dried. "You know my name."

"We know your function."

"You altered the ledger."

"There is no denial. The alteration was sanctioned."

"Sanctioned by whom?"

"Authority beyond your species."

Ardent's voice sharpened. "You expect us to repay debts we are forbidden to remember."

"Understanding the debt is not a prerequisite for repayment."

"We are not children."

"In moral maturity," the Custodian replied, "you have not yet begun adolescence."

The words struck deeper than insult.

They felt diagnostic.

"What happens in seven cycles?"

"Threshold."

"And if we fail?"

"Reclamation."

"Reclamation of what?"

"Meaning."

The room seemed to tilt. Ardent gripped the desk.

"Meaning is not finite," he whispered.

"It becomes finite when abused."

"Who abused it?"

"Your signer believed your species would mature faster."

"My signer," Ardent repeated. "Name them."

"Sealed."

"Why?"

"The truth would destabilize your narrative."

Life left the room for a second. He understood in that moment that humanity's self image was not simply incomplete.

It was engineered.

The Custodian's form flickered. Pressure built around Ardent's skull, then vanished.

"You have been warned."

And it was gone.

Ardent stood shaking. Not from fear.

From certainty.

THE AUDITOR WHO COULD HAVE STOPPED

He stared at the empty space. He could have turned off the console. He could have walked outside, blended into the crowds, allowed himself the ordinary ignorance the universe offered.

Instead, he opened another file.

Personnel records. He filtered for auditors assigned to species with concealed ledgers.

Names appeared. Dozens. Hundreds across centuries.

Terminated.

Reassigned.

Disappeared.

He rubbed his temples. His dream columns now felt prophetic. Those auditors had seen the gaps and followed them.

They had not returned.

His pulse quickened. He was joining a lineage of people who asked questions and ceased to exist.

He wondered if Seren knew.

He wondered if she would mourn him.

He despised himself for caring.

Yet he cared.

He returned to the screen.

Patterns did not lie.

People did.

THE TEN PILLARS BEGIN

He accessed the Bureau's ethics codex. Layers of authorization peeled away. The symbols emerged. Ten Pillars of Meaning Compliance.

The first three glowed.

Pillar One: Intention Transparency

The motives behind action define the moral weight of action. Hidden intention violates universal trust.

Pillar Two: Consciousness Non Exploitation

Identity, memory, emotion, and belief are sovereign resources. Their manipulation incurs debt.

Pillar Three: Debt of Origin

Knowledge acquired without cost or provenance demands future payment.

Ardent stared. Humanity had violated all three.

He scrolled.

The fourth pillar flickered.

Redacted.

His breath shortened.

"What rule reveals what we owe?"

He could not see the answer, but he sensed its weight. Something beyond knowledge. Something involving origin. Something humanity had once possessed and surrendered.

He leaned back. His vision blurred.

Seren Hale's voice floated into memory.

"Truth is costly."

He wondered if she had ever seen the fourth pillar.

He wondered what it had cost her.

THE COORDINATES OF DEBT

His console pulsed.

A message.

We passed once. The cost was unbearable.

Then a string of timestamps. Encoded. He recognized the rhythm. Navigation values hidden within audit references.

He decoded the sequence. The coordinates pointed toward an unlisted region.

The map flickered.

A name appeared.

Edelon

It vanished, replaced by a blank space labeled unregistered.

He whispered it aloud.

"Edelon."

The forgotten colony. The one who had paid.

He opened a reply window.

"Who are you and what was the payment?"

Static. Then:

We are what remained.

The channel closed.

His skin prickled. Humanity had survived a previous reckoning. But not intact.

What did Edelon lose?

Memory?

Purpose?

Soul?

He needed to know.

THE LEAVE REQUEST

He opened a personal interface he had never used.

Leave.

Family matters.

The lie sat on the screen. He waited for rejection.

Approval flashed.

Five days.

Not nearly enough. But enough to disappear.

He encrypted the coordinates. The violation felt like oxygen for the first time in his life.

THE BURDEN OF WANT

He stood in the quiet apartment. The city murmured far below. Ships traced luminous arcs across the sky. Everything seemed fragile now. Measured. Conditional.

He thought of Seren again.

He should not have thought of her. He should have severed the memory.

Instead he whispered a confession no one would hear.

"I want her to understand."

He closed his eyes.

"I want her to know I did not choose ignorance."

He did not understand when desire had become defiance. He only knew it had.

He turned back to the coordinates.

Edelon waited.

The hidden columns formed a path, not merely a mystery.

He whispered one final oath:

"I will audit the truth."

He felt something inside him shift.

Not rebellion.

Purpose.

Not assigned.

Chosen.

And the universe trembled at the change.

CHAPTER THREE

HUMANITY'S BLIND SPOT

Ardent Voss arrived at the transit station two hours before departure, which was an admission of fear he chose not to acknowledge.

The station rose above Virellen's upper atmosphere like a web of glass and light. Docking rings circled its core in slowly rotating layers, each one lit by pale blue beacons that pulsed in steady intervals. From a distance, the structure looked delicate, fragile even, as if one stray gravitational tug would scatter it. Up close, it felt monolithic, a cathedral to movement.

Transit corridors arched overhead in transparent tunnels, allowing travelers to see freighters gliding past, their hulls glowing with faint embers as they aligned for jumps. People moved in steady currents through the concourses, luggage hovering behind some of them in obedient formation. Voices overlapped. Vendors called out drink options. Navigation screens shimmered with route maps and estimated arrivals.

The terminal hummed with life.

Engines thrummed beneath the platforms. Announcements filled the air with that calm, carefully modulated tone that made everything seem predictable, safe, ordinary.

Nothing was safe.

Not anymore.

Ardent moved through the crowd with a deliberate ease he did not feel. His gaze swept over security drones, scanning towers, and discreet Bureau relay nodes embedded in the ceiling. The Bureau was never fully absent from hubs like this. Its presence lingered within the systems that tracked identity, access, and compliance.

He knew what he was doing.

He was still leaving anyway.

His approved leave request sat in the system like a borrowed shield. On the surface, he was a mid level auditor taking permitted time away. No one here had reason to question that. Yet every instinct told him Seren Hale would not let his departure pass without scrutiny.

Seren saw more than most. She always had.

He checked the corridor once more, watching for familiar faces, Bureau insignia, or that particular stillness that preceded official intervention. Nothing. Just travelers, station staff, and the controlled chaos of departure.

His posture remained relaxed. Inside, his thoughts moved like a second heartbeat.

If Seren suspected, how would she move? Would she summon him in quietly? Would she send a formal recall? Or would she simply let him walk and observe what he did next?

Knowing her, she might choose the last option.

That unsettled him more than open confrontation would have.

He reached the boarding gate. His identity marker updated silently in the system, shifting his designation from active auditor to civilian traveler. He felt the change as a subtle jolt within his neural implant, as if a thread connecting him to the Bureau's central consciousness had loosened.

For the first time in years, he was leaving Bureau territory without a Bureau assignment.

It felt like stepping off the edge of a ledger that had always told him where to place his feet.

Five days. That was his window.

He hoped it was enough.

THE ILLUSION OF CHOICE

The shuttle assigned to his first leg of travel was a mid range vessel designed for regional routes between orbital nodes. It gleamed with clean lines and soft illumination, giving the impression of comfort and simplicity. Ardent knew better. These vessels were as regulated as any Bureau facility. Every surface hid sensors. Every seat tracked biometric patterns.

He had planned for that.

The shuttle would take him to a larger hub. From there he would slip into a longer route under a second identity, one that existed only in shallow registers and did not link back to his auditor credentials.

The transit staff scanned his travel token with polite indifference. The Bureau's affiliation flag still stood next to his name, even though he had not explicitly used it. Their posture shifted almost imperceptibly. People treated auditors as if they carried a quiet contagion. No one wanted trouble from the Bureau, and auditors were trouble given human shape.

He stepped through the scanner frame. A thin beam of light swept over his body. He kept his expression neutral.

He knew what the scanner could detect. Unauthorized data storage. Restricted encryption keys. Suspicious neural overlays. The Edelon coordinates pulsed in the hidden layer of his implant, buried beneath decoy codes and harmless clutter he had padded around them.

The frame chimed once.

Clear.

The gate flashed green. The transit officer offered a practiced smile and a gesture toward the boarding ramp.

Ardent exhaled in a slow, silent breath and stepped aboard.

The cabin was arranged in staggered rows. Some passengers laughed as they stowed their bags. Others argued mildly about seating. One couple took pictures of themselves with the planet framed in the window behind them. For them, this journey might mark a vacation or a family reunion.

Ardent watched them for a moment, then turned toward his assigned seat.

He chose a place by the window.

Outside, the docking collar retracted. The shuttle eased away from the station with the grace of practiced precision. Gravity fields adjusted. Virellen filled his view, clouds spiraling over its luminous oceans. The planet radiated confidence. Towers reached upward from its continents. Transit lines gleamed like circuitry across its surface.

Humanity looked like a species in control of its destiny.

Ardent had begun to see something else.

Destiny, he now understood, was not the same as purpose.

Purpose could be chosen.

Destiny had been borrowed.

He remembered the hidden ledger.

License of ascension. Collateral. Human essence.

He pressed his palm lightly against the window. The transparent surface felt colder than it should have.

"Who taught us to believe we were chosen?" he whispered.

The question tasted bitter.

He had been raised on the narrative that progress came from effort and resilience. Humanity had earned its place among the stars by enduring hardship and pushing boundaries. He had never questioned that story. Why would he? It made suffering meaningful.

The hidden columns told a different version.

Someone had accelerated humanity's rise. The Exchange had granted knowledge and technology far beyond the natural pace of development. In return, humanity had given something foundational it no longer remembered losing.

A child given a weapon does not question who paid for it.

He swallowed.

"What did we pay to feel special?" he asked softly.

There was no answer in the cold glass, only the reflection of a man who suddenly realized how small his understanding had been.

THE DOCTRINE OF ENTITLEMENT

The shuttle docked at the central hub with subtle metallic thuds, locking into a larger ring that circled the station's heart. Here, trade routes intersected in a complex web. Gates opened onto vessels headed toward dozens of worlds.

The hub was massive. Its transit concourse stretched outward in a spiraling pattern, each branch dedicated to a particular region. Holographic displays floated above walkways, projection after projection celebrating human accomplishment.

Worlds colonized.

Technologies developed.

Art forms invented.

Philosophies debated.

Every projection carried a quiet subtext.

Humanity is remarkable.

Humans paused beneath the displays, some pointing with pride. Children pressed their hands against the shimmering images of distant colonies they might one day visit.

Ardent walked among them, feeling as though he had stepped into a museum of carefully curated illusions. He recognized the psychological design now. None of this was accidental.

The architecture of the hub reinforced the story of human exceptionalism. Every corridor contained subtle visual cues. Ascending lines. Expanding patterns. Rising arches.

Progress was baked into the walls.

He stopped before a sculpture in the main hall. A hand carved from white stone reached upward, holding a torch of golden light. The torch emitted a soft radiance that warmed the faces of those who passed beneath it.

A plaque at the base read:

We ascend because we dare.

Ardent frowned.

There was no mention of anything else.

No hint that the ascent had been facilitated, measured, and charged.

There was a line missing.

We ascend because we dared.

We remain because we paid.

He doubted that version would ever be installed.

Ignorance here was not an oversight. It was scaffolding. A species that viewed itself as inherently chosen would never think to ask who had done the choosing.

People who believe they are owed something never look for the invoice.

He turned away from the sculpture, tension creeping into his shoulders. The Bureau had not invented human arrogance. It had harnessed it.

He thought of Seren.

He wondered if she saw this place the way he was seeing it now, as an elaborate narrative structure meant to keep humanity docile. Or did she still believe she was merely preserving order?

He remembered the look on her face during the hearing. Calm, but not indifferent. That pause before she told him ignorance protected survival.

Did she know the full truth of the debt?

Or was she, like him until recently, enforcing rules written long before her birth?

A part of him wanted to talk to her. To show her what he had found. To watch comprehension unfold in her eyes.

Another part of him knew that if she understood, she might be the one ordered to stop him.

And she would obey.

Because Seren Hale had been built to protect systems, not individuals.

He hated that he was not sure whether he resented that or admired it.

THE FORBIDDEN ORIENTATION

He purchased a ticket to a long range cruiser under a false name. The transaction passed through without friction. The system accepted the alias because it resembled a legitimate Bureau identity format. He felt a faint chiming in his implant as the new paper trail attached itself to his neural signature.

He moved to a quieter section of the concourse to wait for boarding.

The crowd's noise faded as he stepped into a side corridor lined with maintenance consoles. Most travelers ignored this area. There were no bright projections here, only status monitors and access ports for station staff.

His implant pinged.

A fragment of corrupted data rose into his perception like a bubble emerging from deep water. It shimmered at the edge of his consciousness, labeled as residual training material.

That was odd.

He focused on it.

The fragment expanded, revealing a file header.

Orientation Directive 0.

Ardent stilled.

Orientation files did not begin at zero. Orientation One was standard Bureau introduction for new auditors. Two and Three covered Ethics Application and Cross Species Compliance.

Zero implied something else.

Foundations.

Precedent.

Origin.

He hesitated.

If he opened it, he crossed another line.

If he did not, he went blindly toward a mystery that might already have an answer.

His hand rested on the maintenance console as if to steady himself. He granted the file access.

The corridor darkened. The air around him shifted as his implant linked to the local holo projectors. Light poured outward, rearranging itself into a scene.

The Bureau's atrium appeared, but not as he currently knew it. The walls were raw stone instead of polished material. No silence regulators. No soft light. Workers spoke openly. The sound of their voices echoed.

Four figures stood before a gathering of early auditors.

Their faces were blurred, but their names appeared in sharp clarity beneath them.

Veda Arkan.

Torren Halix.

Seraph Jin.

Miren Voss.

Ardent felt his chest tighten.

Voss.

The name settled in him like a weight. He did not know enough of his own family line to trace it, but the possibility of connection suddenly felt uncomfortably real.

A voice addressed the assembled crowd. It seemed to come from all four founders at once.

"This is Orientation Directive Zero. This file is reserved for those who must understand why the Bureau exists before they swear to serve it."

Scenes unfolded.

Earth engulfed in storms. Cultures collapsing under the weight of competing worldviews. Plagues fueled not merely by biology, but by distorted belief. Movements that began with hope dissolved into fanaticism.

Humanity had weaponized meaning against itself.

Then another image.

A presence descending into that chaos, not as a ship, not as a god, but as an arrangement of offer and acceptance. The Exchange.

It approached humanity with a simple proposition.

You are destroying yourselves with unregulated purpose.

We will halt your collapse.

We will lend you stability, knowledge, and guidance.

In return, you will put your meaning under escrow.

The terms unfolded in text.

License of ascension.

Collateral: cognitive potential.

Collateral: memory of origin.

Collateral: human essence, divisible.

The young auditors in the projection shifted uneasily.

Veda Arkan stepped forward.

"Trade creates obligations," she said. "Obligations without structure create ruin. The Exchange has agreed to lend what we lacked. We must ensure the debt is honored."

Torren Halix added, "We will measure not only what we receive, but how we think, choose, and desire. Intention will be quantified. Motive will be tracked."

Seraph Jin lifted a crystalline object. Within it, colors shifted.

"Meaning is the most volatile resource in existence," she said. "We will regulate its growth."

Finally, Miren Voss spoke.

Her voice was the quietest, yet it carried furthest.

"Existence is not free," she said. "Purpose is collateral. Our species will forget this. That forgetting is part of the contract. We will remember for them. Our duty is not to protect humanity from external threat. Our duty is to ensure humanity never becomes a threat to the structure of meaning itself."

The room in the projection fell silent.

Words appeared in the air above them, and above Ardent where he stood in the corridor.

Mandate of the First Moderators.

Humanity must never again define its own cosmic purpose without oversight.

The Exchange reserves the right to reclaim collateral if repayment fails.

The Bureau will suppress any origin story that leads to independent meaning.

Awareness of the first debt constitutes destabilizing knowledge.

The Bureau does not serve humanity. The Bureau serves the balance of meaning.

The projection intensified for a moment, then faded.

Orientation Directive Zero concluded with a final sentence.

Ignorance is the shield. Meaning is the risk. We are the accountants of existence.

The display dissolved. The maintenance corridor reappeared. Distant transit announcements resumed their rhythm.

Ardent stood motionless.

His heart felt like a lodged stone.

The Bureau had not been created by humanity to manage trade.

Humanity had been allowed to create it as a condition of survival.

The founders had not simply been administrators.

They had been negotiators in a bargain that mortgaged every future generation.

He realized something else in that moment.

If Seren Hale had reached her rank, she had likely seen this orientation.

She knew what he had just learned.

She had lived with it longer.

He tried to imagine what that did to a mind. To carry the knowledge that your entire species existed on conditional terms. That your job was to keep everyone else ignorant of that condition.

He felt a strange surge of sympathy that he quickly crushed.

He did not have time for sympathy.

But the thought remained.

Seren had been obeying an impossible mandate.

And he was about to break it.

SEREN HALE: THE AUDITOR WHO LEFT

On Helios Spire, Seren Hale stood alone in a darkened observatory, watching the streams of data rolling across the vaulted display.

The station floated above Virellen in a controlled orbit, but the Bureau's reach extended far beyond that. From here, she could see transit logs, authorization changes, and patterns of movement that most people never realized were monitored.

Her eyes caught on one entry.

Ardent Voss.

Leave approved.

Destination profile: ambiguous.

She moved her hand along a control strip. The display zoomed in on his recent activity. His access logs flickered into view.

An obsolete forensic tool.

Restricted ethics codex queries.

Unusual access to structural data.

Orientation Directive Zero.

Her jaw tightened.

So he had found it.

Of course he had.

Ardent Voss possessed the kind of mind that could not leave a pattern unresolved. It had been why she had flagged him for advancement years ago. It was also why he now posed a risk.

She closed her eyes briefly.

She could still picture him in his first year at the Bureau. Sitting at a console much too large for his rank, leaning forward with that perpetual focus, as if the world might fall apart if he looked away.

He had impressed her even then.

Not because he worked hard. Many did.

Because he sought structure beneath structure. Because he treated every inconsistency as a thread leading somewhere intolerable.

Because he reminded her of herself before the orientation file of her own training had shown her the weight of the bargain.

She remembered the first time she had heard his name. A junior auditor who had identified a motive inconsistency in a minor planetary case that senior staff had missed. When she reviewed his work, she had seen it instantly.

Here is someone you can use.

Here is someone you must watch.

Over time she had come to know the shape of his thinking. She knew when he would question a directive, when he would press too far, when he would bite back his doubt and obey.

She had also noticed the way his gaze lingered on her face a fraction longer than necessary when they spoke.

She pretended not to notice.

Attachment was a danger she could not afford. He was a subordinate. A junior officer. A gifted analyst. He was not supposed to be anything else.

Yet when she told him truth was more costly than belief, and saw the hurt behind his eyes, she had felt a small fracture inside herself.

He had signed the same oath she had.

He had not known what she knew then.

He knew now.

The display in front of her pulsed again. Transit data updated. His shuttle had departed. He was now en route to a regional hub, then beyond.

She could call for his recall. She could issue a quiet notice to local enforcement to detain him for questioning. She could restrict his identity marker and trap him in any station he entered.

She did none of those things.

Instead, she watched his trajectory and thought of Orientation Directive Zero.

There had been a line in it that had never left her.

Awareness of the first debt constitutes destabilizing knowledge.

Seren had built her life around containing that destabilization.

Now Ardent carried it within him.

She asked herself a question she had not permitted before.

How much of my loyalty is duty, and how much is fear?

The answer did not come.

Her thoughts drifted back to the last look he had given her in the hearing room. Not hatred. Not defiance.

Something like disappointment.

She exhaled and opened a secure channel.

"Custodian liaison," she said. "Flag auditor Ardent Voss as a variable of interest. Do not intercept without my authorization."

A mechanical voice acknowledged.

"Variable monitored. No intervention initiated."

She closed the channel.

Seren Hale stood in the hush of the observatory and admitted silently, if only to herself:

"I do not want him to die for asking the right questions."

She turned back to the data.

The universe cared nothing for what she wanted.

But she did.

And that, she realized, was its own quiet rebellion.

A MESSAGE WITHOUT ORIGIN

On the long range cruiser that carried him away from the hub, Ardent found a seat near the rear. The cabin lights dimmed. A display screen unrolled across the length of the ceiling.

A documentary began.

Humanity's Dawn.

He had seen it before.

Ancient humans crouched in caves. Storms raged. Fire was discovered. Language emerged. Tools and art followed in rapid succession. Cities appeared. Empires rose.

The narrator spoke of ingenuity, resilience, and imagination.

Ardent watched with a tightening jaw.

The leaps were too abrupt. Knowledge appeared without a traceable line of experimentation. Myths spoke of beings who descended from the sky and imparted wisdom, then departed. He had once found these stories charming, the poetic exaggerations of early humanity.

Now he saw the signature of a contract.

Assets granted.

Collateral claimed.

"What makes humanity special," the narrator intoned, "is our ability to dream beyond limitation."

Ardent almost laughed.

Humanity had not dreamed beyond limitation.

The dream had been placed within them.

Someone had lifted the ceiling on what they could imagine, while quietly lowering the floor on what they could remember.

He whispered, "Someone mortgaged our species."

The man in the seat beside him shifted, glancing over with confusion. Ardent turned away, pretending to study the seat interface.

The cabin screens flickered.

Static washed for a second across the projected images. Then the documentary cut out.

Words appeared across every display.

THE AUDIT IS NOT DELAYED.

A ripple of unease moved through the passengers. Murmurs rose.

"Is this part of the program?" someone asked.

"Must be a glitch," another replied.

The message vanished. Humanity's Dawn resumed. The narrator continued as if nothing had occurred.

Ardent's skin prickled.

This was no glitch.

His implant tingled. A new encrypted string appeared at the edge of his awareness. He opened it carefully.

You walk toward truth.

Truth walks toward you.

No sender. No trace.

He closed the file.

Someone had noticed him. Perhaps multiple someones.

He was no longer just an auditor examining a ledger.

He was an anomaly inside someone else's audit.

He sat back as the ship aligned for the jump corridor. Acceleration pressed him into his seat. Stars outside stretched into thin lines of light.

He watched them and understood something with terrifying clarity.

Humanity's greatest flaw was not ignorance.

It was trained blindness.

A species convinced it owed nothing would never prepare for the day repayment was demanded.

The cruiser entered the corridor. Space folded. Engines roared with carefully modulated force.

Ardent closed his eyes.

He saw columns with missing foundations.

He saw founders who had traded memory for survival.

He saw Seren Hale, standing in a room of data, watching him leave and making her own terrible calculations.

He whispered into the hum of the jump:

"Something is coming that does not care what we believe. It only cares what we owe."

The universe did not reply.

It did not need to.

The debt was already written.

And for the first time since the contract had been signed, someone was reading it.

CHAPTER FOUR

THE PRICE OF IGNORANCE

The transport vessel fell out of the jump corridor with a deep, shuddering groan that moved through the hull like a living thing. For a heartbeat the artificial gravity lost its grip and everyone on board floated half a breath above their seats before the systems caught up and dragged them gently back down.

A murmur passed through the cabin. Safety harnesses clicked. Fabric rustled. The tired rustle of people who believed travel was routine and the universe was known.

Ardent Voss did not move.

He sat very still, eyes fixed on the viewport beside him.

There was nothing.

No beacon lattice. No silver threads of trade routes. No faint haze of traffic, no soft halos of stations or platforms or relay nodes. The familiar architecture of civilized space was gone.

Outside the glass waited a black so complete it seemed to devour even the memory of light. It was not the rich, textured darkness he knew, the kind laced with distant stars and nebulae. This was a flat, soundless absence. A field of denial.

The navigation overlay at the edge of the viewport insisted there should be light here. Identifiers marked the positions of stars the eye could not see. Ellipses traced orbits that had nothing visible in them. A ghost map of a sky that had been removed.

The coordinates he had decoded from the hidden message had led them here, to a region the Bureau classified as Unregistered Zone E P Zero One. On the system map, it appeared as a clean, uninterrupted void.

As if someone had scraped stars from the fabric of space and polished the gap smooth.

Ardent released a slow breath. The faint mist of it touched the viewport and vanished.

This was the first time he had seen deliberate absence at cosmic scale.

He knew the patterns of erasure in data. Missing epochs in a ledger. Transactions cut out and resewn. Columns with gaps where numbers should be. Those were abstractions, marks on a surface.

This was the same act performed on the sky.

It felt wrong in a way that had nothing to do with fear and everything to do with balance. It offended the part of his mind that expected continuity, that trusted the universe to at least keep its own accounting intact.

He folded his hands together to keep them from shaking.

Where the Stars Should Be

A burst of static crackled through the vessel's intercom, followed by the pilot's voice, flattened by the cabin speakers.

"Arrival at outer boundary. Stand by for clearance request."

Clearance, Ardent thought. From whom.

The Bureau did not patrol this region. Its jurisdiction ended at the last registered outpost. No known species had claimed this coordinate block. Trade lanes curved deliberately around it like arteries avoiding scar tissue.

Unless the Exchange sat here, outside of maps.

He glanced at the cabin display panel. A simple status line pulsed at the top.

Awaiting response.

Minutes stretched in artificial air. Someone in the back coughed. A child asked if they were there yet and was shushed quickly. A man three rows ahead let out a shaky laugh and said something about atmospheric interference. His seatmate suggested there must be a glitch in the starfield projection.

As if the universe had simply failed to load.

Ardent knew better.

The Exchange did not glitch. It did not forget. It did not misplace stars. When it removed something, there was a reason, and that reason was always written somewhere, even if the script had been buried.

He watched the status line pulse.

Awaiting response.

Awaiting response.

Awaiting response.

The display flickered.

Entry denied. Authority code: Not recognized.

The words appeared in calm neutral text, as though refusing them entrance to an erased portion of space were no more significant than denying a docking request.

From the front of the cabin came a hissed curse. The deck vibrated as the pilot attempted manual override. The faint rising hum of secondary systems spun up, then flattened again when the command failed.

Then the stars changed.

A Gate of Logic

A thread of light appeared in the void, so thin at first that Ardent thought it a sensor artifact. It sharpened, brightened, and then split, as if the darkness itself were a membrane parting along a precise incision.

Out of that cut a shape unfolded.

It had no engines. No visible matter. It was not a ship. It was a configuration, a geometric command impressed upon reality. Lines drew themselves from nothing and locked into place, meeting at angles that made his eyes ache if he stared too long. Each segment glowed with a pale, steady radiance that had nothing to do with reflection and everything to do with intention.

The structure hung there like a judicial seal pressed into the night.

A Custodian Gate.

The word rippled through the cabin. A whisper here, a gasp there. Someone crossed themselves with a gesture from an old planetary faith. Someone else whispered that it had to be a simulation, that the Exchange would never show itself to a civilian transport.

Ardent stood without realizing he was standing.

The Exchange had noticed.

The Gate did not move. It did not emit weapons or extend docking arms. It simply existed, and that existence felt like a verdict.

The surface of the structure shifted. Symbols rose like embossed script from a metal plate, only this was not metal and the symbols were not any language he had been born into. They were ledger glyphs. Terms. Ratifications. Entire contracts reduced to minimal strokes and curves.

This was the script of the Exchange itself.

At the front of the cabin, the pilot transmitted identity signatures. Vessel registry. Passenger manifest. Bureau affiliations. Every credential human systems recognized as legitimate.

The Gate did nothing.

The glyphs turned upon themselves in silent calculation.

Then they reassembled into words the human mind could process.

HUMAN ENTRY IS RESTRICTED.

The text appeared on the forward viewport, vast and unavoidable.

The reaction in the cabin was confusion, not terror. These passengers believed in safety nets, not in existential debt. They had Bureau identity tags. Insurance provisions. Rights.

"What does that mean restricted."

"Is this one of those drills."

"Maybe the Exchange is updating something."

Ardent's chest felt tight.

This was not a blockade of travel.

It was a blockade of access to record.

Something beyond that border belonged to an account humanity was not allowed to see.

He knew that flavor of prohibition from data work. There were files marked sensitive, sealed, classified. This felt different. The Gate did not simply hide. It denied that any legitimate human claim existed here at all.

He swallowed.

Some part of him, older than training, wanted to turn back. Another part, the part that hated gaps in columns and missing entries, leaned closer to the glass.

He whispered one name.

"Edelon Prime."

The sound of it barely reached his own ears, yet the Gate responded.

The glyphs spun, rearranged themselves, and settled into new words.

YOU WERE NOT INVITED.

His breath caught.

Not humanity.

You.

Something on the other side recognized his presence as a single mind, not as a passenger in a crowd.

Ardent sat down slowly.

He could feel the blood moving in his fingertips.

The text changed again, as if the structure were thinking.

TURN BACK. NOTHING HERE IS OWED TO YOU.

There was a flaw in that, as clean and small as a misaligned digit on a balance sheet.

If nothing here was owed, then something had once existed to make that statement true. No one declared nothingness in a place that contained only emptiness. You declared nothing where there had been something that was now forbidden.

Someone had decided humans must not see the balance.

He heard his own voice. It sounded smaller than he expected.

"Show me what is beyond."

For a moment the Gate froze. Not in movement, since it had none, but in some deeper posture. The glyphs ceased their subtle, constant adjustment. The light steadied.

Then the reply appeared.

YOU CANNOT AFFORD IT.

The words lay in front of him like a closed door.

The Passenger Who Was Not

Before the tension in the cabin could resolve into panic, another voice spoke.

"That is not entirely true."

It came from the far end of the aisle. Calm. Unhurried. Spoken at a conversational volume that somehow cut through overlapping murmurs and the low hum of systems.

Ardent turned.

A man stood near the emergency hatch. He leaned against the frame in a posture that seemed relaxed, yet the space around him did not agree. The air wavered. The lighting bent slightly at his edges, as if photons were not certain whether they should acknowledge him.

Ardent tried to recall seeing him board. A memory should have been there, a simple image of a face in a boarding line, a shape moving through a corridor.

Nothing surfaced.

Passengers near the hatch shifted without realizing it, leaving a subtle arc of space around him. Their eyes brushed past his outline, skated away, and landed on safer objects. Seatbacks. Screens. Their own hands.

Ardent felt the wrongness of it settle in his bones.

"Who are you," he asked.

The man smiled. It was not a hostile expression, but there was no warmth in it, no shared humanity. It was an acknowledgement of social expectation performed without conviction.

"Someone who remembers."

His voice carried no accent Ardent could place, yet it felt old. Not in sound, but in the way it wore the words, as if language were something it had practiced long after it ceased to need it.

"You are from Edelon," Ardent said.

The man inclined his head.

"We once paid what humanity owed," he replied. "We survived the Audit."

The word survived sounded like an error when paired with his eyes.

Ardent's throat tightened.

"At what cost."

The man's gaze shifted to the viewport, to the silent Gate, then back to Ardent. In that movement there was a depth like a well whose bottom had been removed.

"The price was not measured in blood," he said. "The Exchange never takes what can be replaced."

Ardent thought of other debtor worlds in the records. Wars. Famine. Population collapses. All terrible, all measurable in bodies. All things that could, in theory, be rebuilt.

He swallowed.

"So what did it take," he asked.

The man studied him for a moment, as if deciding whether Ardent possessed the vocabulary to understand the answer.

"When a species is young," he said quietly, "it loves its flaws. It writes them into stories and songs. It calls them character. It builds pantheons around them. Recklessness becomes courage. Impulse masquerades as destiny. The belief that the self is sacred grows faster than wisdom."

He took a small step closer. The air seemed to thin around him.

"The Exchange took our certainty," he said. "It took our belief that our choices belonged to us."

Ardent felt a sensation like a drop in pressure inside his chest.

He thought of what made a person a person. Memory. Preference. Obligation. The felt sense that the next decision was theirs, even if constrained.

Edelon had kept its bodies, its infrastructure, its language.

But not its sense of inner ownership.

"We live," the man continued. "We breathe. We retain information. We can recite history, list events, describe everything that happened."

He lifted his hand and tapped his temple lightly.

"But we no longer feel that those things are ours. We exist as participants in a story that continues without the conviction that we are its authors."

His eyes met Ardent's fully now.

"That is what the Exchange takes when a debtor passes without maturity. Not life. Not mind. Self."

Ardent's mouth felt dry.

"You are alive and empty," he whispered.

For a fraction of a second, something like pain crossed the man's face, too fast to hold.

"Debt repaid," he said.

The Gate Opens

No one else reacted.

A woman across the aisle shifted to adjust her harness and glanced right through the man as if he were a trick of light. A child pulled at a parent's sleeve and asked why the stars were gone. The parent answered with a distraction about navigation while the Gate filled the sky in front of them.

Reality itself had filtered the conversation. Only Ardent received it.

The Gate pulsed.

The geometric lines brightened, then folded inward, not physically, but conceptually. Space along its inner axis contracted, then hollowed out. What had been a flat plane of light now held depth, a corridor carved into nothing.

It reminded Ardent of a ledger page bending at one line, revealing a space between entries where something had been hidden.

The pilot's voice came through, unsteady.

"Gate is opening. We have clearance to proceed."

Ardent stared at the corridor.

This was not clearance. Not in the sense the Bureau understood it. This felt like a door being opened by something that owned the house, not because it welcomed guests, but because it was letting a creditor in.

He shook his head.

The stranger turned back to the viewport. The pale light from the Gate washed across his face and revealed, just for a moment, how tired he was. Not physically. Existentially. As if continuing to exist without ownership of that existence had worn him thin.

"Your species believes it earned progress," he said. "That belief is your cage."

His gaze slid toward the ceiling, toward the unseen bureaucratic lattices where Bureau signals passed and Exchange monitors watched.

"The Bureau exists to maintain that belief. Memory of origin was collateral. Purpose was the loan."

Purpose. Not effort. Not achievement. The very sense that living had direction.

He fixed his eyes on Ardent again.

"You are the first auditor who has looked for the missing columns."

Ardent felt his own voice tremble.

"Why help me," he asked.

The man's expression changed by degrees. Something softer tried to surface through the vacancy. It did not quite make it, but the attempt itself was terrible to witness.

"Because we are what you will become," he said, "if you pass without understanding the price."

He stepped back toward the emergency hatch. His outline began to blur, not like mist, but like an equation being erased.

"Go to Edelon," he said. "See what we paid. Then decide if humanity deserves to remain."

His final words hung in the air like dust motes in a shaft of light.

"Truth is not owed. It is earned."

Then he was gone.

No displacement of air. No flicker in the lights. He simply was not there, in the same way the stars were not there beyond the Gate.

The structure remained open. Its corridor waited, a straight passage into corrected history.

The Gate did not close.

It waited.

Ardent sat slowly, aware of his heart beating too fast. His hands trembled against the armrests. Around him, passengers murmured about how beautiful the phenomenon was, how rare, how fortunate they were to see a Custodian structure up close.

They did not realize it had looked directly at them and found them irrelevant.

For the first time, Ardent understood something that went beyond horror.

The Exchange did not care whether humanity lived.

It cared whether the terms of the contract were honored.

Death was an incidental outcome.

The true punishment was emptiness.

Meanwhile, on Helios Spire

Light from a simulated starfield washed across the curved glass of the observatory on Helios Spire. Lines of traffic arced in graceful loops above Virellen, streaks of silver and gold against the velvet black. Cargo ships slid between platforms. Shuttles leapt from orbit to atmosphere.

Seren Hale stood alone before the main display.

The room was quiet, insulated from station noise. In the stillness, the hum of processors and the soft tick of system recalibrations sounded almost like breathing.

On the central console in front of her, a thin line traced the course of a much smaller ship, one that moved away from all the busy, crowded light.

Civilian Transport Serynth.

Destination: Unregistered Zone E P Zero One.

Bureau relevant passenger: Ardent Voss.

His name glowed in a calm, indifferent font.

It should have been a relief to see his trajectory neatly rendered, his path calculable. She had approved his leave request, knowing it was a lie. She had seen through the invented family matter with the same precision she applied to ledger anomalies.

Approval allowed her to keep watching.

Yet the sight of that thin line, heading toward empty space, tightened something in her chest.

A notification pulsed at the edge of her vision.

Supervisor emotional deviation recorded.

She did not open it.

Her reflection in the glass looked exactly as it should. Uniform crisp. Hair ordered. Face composed. No sign of fracture.

Her thoughts did not match.

He should not have gone.

He should not have been able to read Orientation Directive Zero, to bypass archived restrictions, to ask the questions he had asked when he sat in her office and refused to accept partial answers.

And yet.

She had not truly tried to stop him.

Not when he submitted the request. Not when she saw the pattern of his inquiries. Not when she recognized the particular hunger in his eyes, the kind that would always lean toward the missing piece, even if a drop at the edge of the world waited there.

Her fingers hovered over a command in the oversight interface.

She could still flag his leave as irregular. She could mark his last access as a potential breach. She could elevate the case to Enforcement. It would trigger an interception. A shuttle would be dispatched. He could be pulled back before the transport went beyond Bureau reach.

She let her hand fall to her side.

Understanding was a contagion. Once knowledge existed, it wanted to spread. Once a mind learned that the sky could be edited, it would never again trust that stars were just stars.

If Ardent returned with truth, she would not be able to absorb his report as a neutral document. She would have to choose which part of herself to betray.

The Bureau.

Or whatever part of her still believed in him.

For now, she did nothing.

On the display, the Serynth shrank, its icon moving off the edge of familiar grids toward the blank, labeled void.

Seren watched until the ship passed the last registered coordinate.

She told herself it was professional diligence.

The thought that rose underneath did not agree.

He was not just a variable in a ledger. Not just a test particle in a model, drifting toward a controlled anomaly.

He was the first human she had ever feared the universe was not prepared for.

The feeling that rose in her chest at that realization did not belong to the Exchange.

It belonged to her.

She stood there until the starfield display cycled and the station lights dimmed into night mode.

Then she turned away, the soles of her boots soft against the observatory floor, and left the room without acknowledging the second notification that appeared in the corner of her console.

Supervisor deviation escalating.

The Price of Ignorance

Back on the transport, the vessel crossed the boundary.

One moment, the instruments insisted they hovered at the edge of known space. The next, every registered chart revised itself. The unregistered zone accepted their presence into its silent calculus.

The corridor within the Gate stretched ahead of them like an illuminated ledger line, narrow and straight. Outside it, space remained blank and depthless.

Ardent felt the crossing in his body long before the cabin announced it. A slight pressure behind the eyes. A sense that something was taking measure, not of height or weight, but of intention.

Humanity had not merely forgotten its debt.

It had forgotten that purpose itself was collateral.

That existence could be repossessed without touching a single body.

He watched the darkness beyond the lighted corridor and saw Edelon's emissary in his mind, those eyes that remembered information without believing it belonged to him.

He wondered how many times humanity had told itself that it was chosen, special, destined. How many monuments it had built to that conviction. How many histories it had edited so that victory looked inevitable and debt looked like virtue.

The Exchange did not care about any of that.

It cared about the terms.

Ardent Voss sat with his hands still shaking slightly and understood only one clear thing.

Humanity was not moving toward destruction.

Destruction would have been a clean break.

Humanity was traveling steadily toward a due date.

It was not the end of the world.

It was the moment the invoice arrived.

And somewhere ahead, on a world that had already paid, Edelon kept the receipts.

CHAPTER FIVE

THE MISSING MILLENNIA

The vessel descended into Edelon's atmosphere like a blade easing into water. At first the turbulence resembled ordinary atmospheric entry, a pull of gravity against reinforced hull plating. Then the sensation changed. The pressure was not external. It pushed inward, scraping against thought rather than metal. A quiet ache formed at the base of Ardent Voss's skull, tightening as though unseen hands were prying open his mind.

His ears began to ring. The sound was neither high nor low, not mechanical nor organic. It was as if the universe itself had taken a breath and then refused to exhale. The passengers around him shifted, frowning and rubbing their temples. A child whimpered and clung to her mother. The pilot muttered under her breath and attempted to steady the controls, but the ship lurched sideways with an unnatural resistance that did not match any known atmospheric signature.

Ardent closed his eyes. He had studied the Exchange for years, cataloging anomalies with mathematical calm, yet he had never experienced its presence directly. The Exchange was not a force of nature. It did not move planets or break worlds. It moved meaning. It reshaped perception, accounting not for matter, but for the architecture of belief. Entering

Edelon felt like stepping across a threshold where intention had been taxed out of existence.

Then, abruptly, the pressure vanished.

The vessel stabilized with a final shudder. The ringing in Ardent's ears softened and then ceased. The sky outside shifted from darkness into muted gold, a dawn without warmth, a horizon without invitation.

Edelon came into view.

A Civilization Without Identity

Ardent leaned so close to the viewport that his breath fogged the glass. Edelon was not the wasteland he had expected. It was not charred or overgrown. The skyline rose in clean, seamless towers that looked grown rather than built. Roads stretched outward in networks of immaculate white stone. Large communal squares shimmered beneath translucent canopies that gently refracted light.

It was beautiful. It was precise.

It was horrifying.

There were no banners. No symbols. No murals or graffiti hinting at rebellion. No child's scrawl on a wall. No colors chosen for preference. The city was symmetrical without pride, functional without choice. Identity had not been erased in fragments. It had been vacuumed clean, leaving no residue of self.

The stranger's warning echoed through Ardent's memory:

We live. We breathe. We remember facts. We no longer believe they belong to us.

This was a world without self.

The ship drifted toward a reception platform. The pilot announced disembarkation procedures, but her voice trembled, as if she doubted her authority to speak. Passengers moved in silence, their excitement wilted. Ardent watched their eyes glaze ever so slightly. It was not submission. It was something worse. It was the loss of the idea that there was anything to resist.

Edelon did not erase thought.

It erased ownership.

Ardent alone seemed unsettled, nauseated by the contrast between perfection and vacancy. He felt a pressure in his chest, the sort that accompanied funerals, except no one here appeared dead.

They simply appeared unnecessary.

The People of Edelon

Figures approached from across the platform. They walked in step, neither quickly nor slowly. Their garments were made from a fabric neither textured nor smooth, a gray so neutral it failed to cast shadows. Their faces were placid. Their eyes were calm. Yet there was something missing. Something fundamental. Ardent had seen corpses with more presence.

One stepped forward and spoke.

"Welcome. You are safe."

The tone was warm enough to avoid suspicion, but utterly hollow. Not monotone, not robotic. It was the absence of emphasis, a voice that had been disconnected from intent.

Ardent bowed his head slightly.

"I am Ardent Voss. I seek understanding."

The Edelonian blinked once.

"Understanding is permitted. Judgment is not."

Ardent raised an eyebrow.

"Why would I judge you?"

The Edelonian smiled, a perfectly shaped expression with no sentiment behind it.

"All who remember judge. We do not remember."

Ardent felt his breath catch.

"You are aware of what you have lost?"

The person nodded.

"Of course. That is why we do not grieve. Ownership creates comparison. Comparison creates debt. We are free of debt."

The calm in the Edelonian's voice chilled Ardent to the bone. Peace, he realized, was not the absence of conflict. Peace here was the absence of anything to desire or defend.

The Exchange had not punished Edelon.

It had neutered it.

The Hollows

The city streets were immaculate. Trees without fragrance lined walkways without names. Houses stood in perfect rows, each identical, each spotless, each devoid of memory. No toys lay abandoned in yards. No music escaped windows. Every door was open, yet nothing inside spoke of habitation. Rooms contained chairs that supported bodies, beds that cradled sleep, tables that received meals, yet none of these objects bore signs of preference. It was as if the world had been designed for occupants who neither cherished nor rejected anything.

Two Edelonians paused near a courtyard and spoke.

"The weather is consistent today."

"Consistency is good."

They continued walking.

Nothing more followed. No elaboration. No observation. No moment of shared amusement.

Ardent felt dizzy. Language here existed only to confirm equilibrium. It was not communication. It was maintenance. These people were alive without living.

He turned to his guide.

"What do you do? What fills your time?"

The guide smiled with serene emptiness.

"There is no time to fill. Time exists. We exist within it. That is sufficient."

Ardent swallowed hard.

"Do you pursue anything?"

"Pursuit implies deficiency. Deficiency implies imbalance. Balance is peace."

Ardent felt a tremor run through him.

Humanity bickered over meaning. It argued about truth and fought over interpretations of history. It clashed between desire and fear, ambition and regret. He had once believed that instability was evidence of failure.

Now he saw the inverse.

Instability was proof of selfhood.

Edelon had outgrown conflict by amputating the capacity to care.

Seren Hale, Elsewhere

Across space, Seren Hale stood inside a monitoring chamber on Helios Spire. Screens flickered with streams of data that tracked vessel trajectories, emotional patterns, and cognitive flags. One line pulsed red.

Ardent Voss. Emotional variance detected. Cognitive deviation exceeding threshold.

Seren felt something tighten beneath her ribs. She placed her hand against the display. Her reflection stared back at her, composed and unreadable, yet her pulse betrayed her neutrality.

She whispered, though no one was there to hear.

"You should not be doing this alone."

A prompt flashed across her console.

Supervisor sentiment deviation recorded. Report pending.

Seren closed her eyes. She did not care. She did not know when Ardent's name had begun to linger in her thoughts after duty hours. She did not know when she began to fear losing him. She only knew that if he uncovered something the Bureau fought to contain, he would not return the same.

She was afraid of the audit.

She was more afraid of what Ardent might find.

The Archive Without History

The Archive towered above the city like a monument to omniscience. Its walls shimmered with shifting script that refused to resolve into symbols. Ardent entered through doors that responded to his presence, contracting behind him like a throat.

Inside, silence was not an absence of noise. It was a force. It pressed against him, flattening thoughts that tried to rise.

Rows of glowing data columns stretched into infinity. No one tended them. No one consulted them. The Edelonians did not need history. They had facts, but not narrative. Facts without ownership were as empty as rooms without occupants.

Ardent activated a terminal. Information flickered into existence.

Audit metrics. Exchange records. Cultural valuations. Psychological metrics.

And then, the entry he sought:

EDELON PRIME — AUDIT RESULT: PASS

BALANCE CORRECTED VIA CULTURAL FORFEITURE

ASSET TRANSFER: ETHICAL IDENTITY

REPAYMENT COMPLETE. SELF REMOVED. SPECIES RETAINED.

Ardent's heart clenched. The Exchange had not erased Edelon.

It had repossessed Edelon's belief in itself.

Without belief, identity dissolved. Without identity, memory became neutral. Without memory, purpose evaporated.

He stumbled back from the terminal and clung to a column for balance. His own reflection trembled in the luminescent surface, distorted by his ragged breathing.

Humanity had borrowed not tools or territory, but meaning.

Humanity had mortgaged the soul of its future.

The debt was due.

The Whispering Hall

As he left the Archive, Ardent heard something impossible. A whisper. Not flat Edelonian speech. Not maintenance language.

Emotion.

Real cadence.

He followed the sound down a corridor the city seemed to ignore. A pulse glowed faintly at the end of the hall. He pressed his palm against the door.

It opened.

Shadows writhed along the walls like living regret. The room smelled of old memory, as if the air remembered everything the people had forgotten.

A figure stepped forward, eyes bright with anguish and awareness.

"You should not have come here."

The voice carried weight. Pain. Ownership.

Ardent inhaled sharply.

"You remember."

"We are the fragments. Those who resisted the removal. We are the consequences of defiance."

Ardent swallowed.

"What did Edelon pay?"

The figure laughed, a sound so brittle it seemed ready to shatter.

"We did not lose memory. We lost belief. We know what happened. We no longer believe it matters."

Ardent felt a tremor of dread rise from the floor into his bones.

Belief was the currency of existence.

Without belief, life continued.

Meaning did not.

The figure leaned close.

"They will not take your bodies. They will not take your minds. They will take the part of you that says you deserve to breathe."

Ardent staggered backward.

Humanity was not afraid of death.

Humanity was afraid of the day it woke up and felt nothing.

The Exchange did not extinguish civilizations.

It hollowed them.

It reclaimed the right to care.

The figure whispered, almost tenderly,

"We envy you. You still think you matter."

Ardent's pulse thundered in his ears. For the first time, he understood the real danger. The Audit did not threaten extinction.

It threatened irrelevance.

Humanity believed it lived in a universe filled with purpose.

The Audit would reveal the truth.

Purpose was rented.

And the bill was due.

CHAPTER SIX

THE IDENTITY OF THE SIGNER

The door closed behind Ardent Voss without a whisper.

It did not latch. It did not lock. It simply ceased to acknowledge the space behind it, as if reality itself had decided the room no longer had any business with the corridor outside. Ardent stood motionless for a moment, his hand hovering near the seam of the vanished entrance. He half expected it to return at his touch, but the smooth wall offered no hint that a threshold had ever existed.

Silence pressed against him. It was not the silence of abandonment or neglect. It felt purposeful, as though the air waited for something to happen. A presence without a voice. A witness without eyes.

In the center of the chamber stood the console.

It did not look ancient in the way ruins look ancient. It looked endured. Its metallic frame bore scratches that suggested intent rather than accident, like someone had once tried to carve certainty into its surface. The top layer was dulled where countless hands had rested, not in routine operation, but in hesitation, as if every touch was an act of consequence.

Ardent approached slowly.

He had walked through audit rooms before. He had examined corrupted ledgers and seized digital vaults full of hidden transactions. He had interrogated civilizations through the mathematics of their choices. Yet nothing he had encountered prepared him for this.

This console did not store information.

It guarded it.

An input pad rested at the front edge, its shape conforming to no design he recognized. It was not ergonomic or technological. It was ceremonial.

Ardent drew in a breath and exhaled once, steadying himself.

He reached out and touched the pad.

A ripple passed through the console. Not light. Not vibration. Something perceptual. The chamber's dimensions seemed to tilt, as if the room reconsidered its relationship to space. The screen flickered alive, releasing a faint glow that illuminated Ardent's face with cold certainty.

A single prompt appeared in stark text:

REQUEST IDENTITY OF EXCHANGE SIGNER

His heart lurched.

For years, humanity debated whether the Exchange was imposed or chosen. Whether it represented cosmic tyranny or divine inevitability. Whether sentience itself was debt or privilege. Philosophers argued. Clerics sanctified. Scientists dismissed. Politicians concealed.

Yet none of them knew who had signed.

No treaty. No proclamation. No surviving witness.

History began with a silence, and humanity built meaning on top of that silence without ever questioning its foundations.

Now the silence waited for Ardent to ask the question.

He pressed his palm against the input pad. The console did not react immediately. Instead, it hesitated as if contemplating the request. Ardent felt as though he had confessed something without speaking. His pulse quickened.

Then the text shifted:

VERIFICATION REQUIRED: COGNITIVE CLAIM

Ardent read it again, slower.

Verification was not a password. Not a key. Not biometric clearance.

It was belief.

To know the signer, one had to accept the premise that the Exchange was real, binding, and deserved acknowledgment. Knowledge demanded surrender. Information required allegiance.

Ardent swallowed.

He whispered, "I accept the truth of the Exchange."

The words felt like stepping off a cliff.

The console pulsed. The room darkened. The glow from the screen expanded outward until it was no longer light but architecture. Columns rose around him, endless and towering, each etched with symbols he instinctively recognized but could not read.

He was no longer in a room.

He stood inside the ledger.

SEGMENT II — Inside the Ledger

The air thickened around Ardent as the ledger walls solidified into towering structures of light and memory. The chamber no longer felt like a physical room. It felt like an idea given architecture. Shapes floated in the distance, geometric and silent, as though the Exchange had distilled entire civilizations into equations.

Lines of glowing script flowed across the columns. They resembled language, yet carried the cadence of accounting. Words and numerals intertwined, forming unbroken sentences of obligation. Ardent felt something ancient stir inside him, like a long dormant instinct awakening.

Debt was not numbers here.

Debt was history.

Each column contained the spiritual cost of choices made by worlds now forgotten. Transactions flickered in cycles of ascension and collapse. Cultures traded belief for survival. Species bartered memory for technology. Entire planets mortgaged their future to escape their past.

He felt both horror and awe.

Humanity was not alone in its desperation.

Ardent reached out. The nearest column responded to his presence. Symbols rearranged themselves into a legible sequence. They were not written. They were remembered.

He read:

EXISTENCE IS A CREDIT

MEANING IS COLLATERAL

CHOICE INCURS INTEREST

His pulse quickened.

Life itself was not owed. It was issued. Consciousness was a line item. Identity was a negotiable asset.

No one had ever told humanity that existing placed it in deficit.

A voice echoed through the ledger. It was not loud, yet it filled every corner of the construct.

"Curiosity is the first debt."

Ardent spun around.

An Edelonian stood behind him. Unlike the others Ardent had encountered, this one radiated intention. His posture carried conviction, not compliance. His gaze did not drift. It anchored itself on Ardent as though measuring him.

He did not appear hostile.

His presence was worse than hostility.

He cared.

"You should not request what you cannot return," the Edelonian said.

Ardent steadied his breathing. "I need to understand. Humanity deserves to know what we inherited."

The remnant shook his head slowly. "Understanding is not the reward. It is the price."

Ardent frowned. "Knowledge is not debt."

The remnant stepped closer.

"All knowledge is debt. Every truth has a cost. You ask who signed, but you do not ask why the signature was needed."

"I will," Ardent replied. His voice trembled, not from fear, but from conviction. "I am an auditor. My purpose is reconciliation."

The Edelonian laughed softly. It was not amusement. It was pity.

"There is no reconciliation. There is only acknowledgment. The Exchange does not forgive. It collects."

Ardent turned back to the console. The screen shimmered, awaiting his next command.

"I need to know who signed the contract for humanity."

The ledger pulsed. The columns trembled, as though the question disturbed something ancient. Ardent sensed reluctance, not from the remnant, but from history itself.

The light condensed into lines of text.

IDENTITY ACCESS GRANTED

DISPLAYING SIGNER OF CONTRACT

Ardent held his breath.

The letters emerged slowly. They looked alien at first. Then, painfully, they arranged themselves into something human.

HOMO SAPIENS COUNCIL OF SURVIVAL

Ardent blinked. The words blurred. He read them again. They did not change.

A council.

Not a mythic founder. Not a prophet. Not a conqueror.

Humanity itself.

His heartbeat stumbled.

"We chose this?" he whispered.

The remnant nodded. "Your species signed its own limitation. The Exchange did not initiate contact. You did."

Ardent shook his head. "Humanity was primitive. It had no ability to negotiate cosmic contracts."

The console disagreed.

ERA OF SIGNATURE: PRE HISTORIC COLLAPSE

Ardent froze.

Pre historic. Beyond recorded memory. Before language crystallized into permanence. Before myth separated from reality.

"There is no record of a collapse," he whispered.

The remnant's expression tightened.

"You erased it. Not as punishment. As collateral."

The console continued:

CONTRACT PURPOSE: SPECIES PRESERVATION

STATUS AT SIGNING: NEAR EXTINCTION EVENT

Ardent's voice cracked. "We were dying."

"Yes," the remnant replied. "Not allegorically. Not spiritually. Physically. Something hunted you. Something stripped your minds of what they needed to survive. The Exchange intervened."

Ardent felt the room close in. His hands trembled. The columns around him flickered with the weight of it all.

"What did we trade?" he asked, though part of him already knew.

The console delivered the answer with indifferent clarity.

COLLATERAL: MEMORY OF ORIGIN AND MEANING OF SELF

Ardent staggered. He felt his knees weaken. He lowered himself to the floor, breath ragged.

Humanity did not evolve blindly.

Humanity evolved amputated.

The remnant's voice softened.

"You did not lose who you were. You surrendered it."

Ardent pressed a shaking hand against his chest, as if steadying his heart could stabilize his mind.

"We traded our identity for survival."

The remnant nodded once.

"Your ancestors chose ignorance as shelter. They believed future generations would mature and reclaim what was lost."

Ardent looked up slowly.

"They were wrong."

SEGMENT III — The First Payment

Ardent rose slowly. His legs felt as though they belonged to someone else. The ledger walls pulsed with faint luminescence, their flickering glyphs like breaths taken by something ancient and patient. He tried to steady his thoughts, but the truth he had uncovered felt too large to be held by a single mind.

He had always believed that humanity struggled because it lacked information.

Now he understood.

Humanity struggled because it was built on the absence of something it had traded away.

The console pulsed again.

NEW QUERY DETECTED

DO YOU SEEK RECORD OF INITIAL PAYMENT?

Ardent hesitated. His voice emerged as little more than a whisper.

"Yes."

The chamber darkened. The ledger columns twisted into a singular thread of golden light. It stretched across the room, almost like a timeline made of living tissue.

The console translated:

FIRST PARTIAL PAYMENT INITIATED

VARIABLE: MYTHOLOGICAL REVISION

ACTION: ERASE SIGNATURE OF CONTRACT

METHOD: CULTURAL TRANSLATION

Ardent frowned. He leaned closer, unwilling to blink.

"Erase signature of contract?"

The remnant nodded. "A species cannot fear what it does not know. The Council understood this. They traded awareness of the contract for the ability to endure its consequences."

The console elaborated:

IMPLEMENTATION THROUGH MYTH

GLOBAL DISTRIBUTION

RECURRING NARRATIVE PATTERNS ASSIGNED

Ardent's pulse quickened. "Assigned?"

The remnant exhaled, as though releasing a memory made of pain.

"Your species did not invent its oldest stories. It received them."

The golden line fractured into thousands of nodes. Each one displayed an image or symbol Ardent instantly recognized: a great flood, a forbidden fruit, a tower reaching for the heavens, a serpent of knowledge, a god warning mortals of ruin.

Humanity's most sacred, universal stories.

He stepped closer, heart pounding.

"You are saying myth is not metaphor."

"No," the remnant replied. "Myth is residue."

Ardent ran a trembling hand along the glowing thread. His fingers passed through a representation of a broken city, submerged beneath waves.

"This one," he whispered. "Every culture has a flood myth. Why?"

The ledger answered.

ARCHIVE ENTRY CONFIRMED

EVENT TRANSLATION: CONTRACT SEVERANCE

DESCRIPTION: ERASE MEMORY OF PRE HUMAN CIVILIZATION

METHOD: SYMBOLIC DELUGE

PURPOSE: REMOVE RECORD OF ORIGIN

Ardent felt his world tilt.

Humanity had not forgotten where it came from.

Humanity had been made to forget.

He moved to another node. A tree with luminous fruit. Serpents. A guardian that banished mortals.

"Forbidden knowledge," Ardent murmured. "The story of exile. The beginning of shame."

The console pulsed again.

ORIGINAL MEANING: LOSS OF ORIGIN

KNOWLEDGE REMOVED TO PROTECT CONTRACT INTEGRITY

MOTIF: RESPONSIBILITY DENIED

OUTCOME: IGNORANCE ENFORCED

Ardent clenched his jaw.

"All this time, we thought these myths warned us against arrogance."

"They warned you," the remnant said, "that you no longer owned yourselves."

A chill slipped beneath Ardent's skin.

"This was the first payment," he whispered. "Erase the memory of the contract. Erase the memory of who we were. Make the debt forgettable."

The remnant shook his head.

"Not forgettable. Unquestionable. That is why every culture shares the same wounds. They did not evolve independently. They inherited scars."

Ardent stumbled backward, overwhelmed.

"Our ancestors traded away identity and left us stories to prevent us from asking where it went."

"Yes," the remnant replied. "You turned the memory of loss into religion. You worshiped absence. You mistook trauma for ancestry."

The console brightened with a sudden flare.

HUMAN INTERPRETATION ERROR DETECTED

CULTURAL MISALLOCATION: HOPE ASSIGNED TO LOSS

RESULT: PERMANENT DEBT AMNESIA

The words cut deeper than any blade.

Humans had taken the residue of their own forfeiture and turned it into mythic beauty.

They had romanticized their erasure.

Ardent pressed both hands against the console. His breath came in ragged waves.

"Why conceal the truth this way? Why not simply delete it?"

The remnant's voice softened.

"Because deletion invites rediscovery. Concealment births obedience. A lie anchored in story becomes reality."

The ledger dimmed. A final line appeared, stark and merciless.

YOU ARE NOT LOST

YOU ARE COLLATERAL

Ardent sank to his knees.

The chamber seemed to breathe around him, as though the ledger recognized his despair and welcomed it.

His ancestors had not feared death.

They had feared extinction of potential.

They had chosen survival and left their descendants to pay the interest.

Humanity's greatest achievements had been built on a foundation of relinquished identity.

Every breakthrough was a borrowed tool.

Every dream was inherited debt.

He whispered into the quiet:

"We were not meant to ascend."

The remnant crouched beside him.

"You were meant to survive. Ascension was accidental. Debt accelerated your minds. You mistook momentum for destiny."

Ardent wiped tears he did not remember shedding.

"Why tell me this now?"

"Because the ledger has reawakened. Your cycle nears its end. You are the first to ask the right question."

Ardent looked up. The remnant's eyes held something terrible and precious.

"You think your species invented ambition. It did not. Ambition was installed as leverage."

Ardent swallowed.

"So our achievements do not belong to us."

"No. And soon, neither will your meaning."

Ardent closed his eyes as the console flickered a new message.

AUDIT DATE

VERIFIED

SEVEN CYCLES REMAIN

The remnant stood.

"Knowledge is not liberation. It is obligation. Now that you know, you cannot return to ignorance."

Ardent whispered:

"We never grew into the debt. We hid from it."

"And now," the remnant replied, "the debt has come to collect."

SEGMENT IV — The Bureau's Shadow

The chamber door sealed behind Ardent without resistance. The silence pressed against him like a physical weight. His hands trembled as he stepped into the open corridor, but no alarm sounded, no voices questioned him, no protocols demanded justification.

On Edelon, nothing enforced order.

Order existed because nothing remained capable of breaking it.

Ardent steadied himself against a wall. Its surface felt unnaturally smooth, as though crafted without tools, without intent. The architecture radiated an absence of personality, a perfection born not of mastery but of surrender. It was beauty stripped of ownership.

He had just learned who signed the Exchange.

Now he had to decide what that knowledge meant.

The Unseen Ledger

Humanity had not been uplifted by destiny. It had been preserved on credit.

The realization struck him with a bone deep ache. Everything he knew, every innovation, every triumph of civilization, every moment humans believed they had earned their place among the stars was now stained with a truth he wished he could unlearn.

Progress was not achievement.

Progress was collateral.

The echoes of the remnant's final words clung to him like frost.

Knowing the signer does not free you. It binds you.

Ardent walked through Edelon's silent avenues. The citizens moved with smooth, graceful precision, their expressions soft but empty. They greeted him without curiosity. They did not ask his purpose. They did not question his presence.

Peace without ownership.

Survival without identity.

Existence without self.

A cold realization unfurled in him. Edelon had not lost something.

It had given something away.

Humanity had mistaken the Exchange for a gift. Edelon understood the truth.

The Exchange was a loan.

And loans were always collected.

A Shadow from Home

A faint sound broke the monotony of footsteps. A voice carried across the plaza, one that did not belong to Edelon.

"Ardent."

He turned faster than he meant to.

She stood at the edge of the platform, framed by Edelon's pale horizon. Seren Hale. Her Bureau uniform remained immaculate, but her presence seemed strained, almost brittle, as if she was holding herself together through discipline alone.

He had never seen her hesitate.

That alone terrified him.

"Seren? How did you get here?"

Her reply carried no anger, only quiet inevitability.

"You think I would let you cross into forbidden space without oversight?"

Ardent felt heat rise in his chest.

"This was never your jurisdiction."

Seren approached. Each step seemed weighted with invisible cost.

"It is now."

Ardent searched her expression. Her eyes were still sharp, still disciplined, but there was something new in them. Not doubt. Not fear.

Recognition.

"You knew something," he said. "Not everything, but enough."

She did not deny it.

"I knew the Bureau was not created for governance. It was created for containment."

Ardent exhaled sharply.

"Containment of what?"

"Truth," Seren replied. "Truth is volatile. It destabilizes belief, and belief sustains the Exchange. If humanity remembers too soon, we rupture the contract."

Her voice softened.

"You were never meant to ask who signed it."

Ardent felt bitterness gather like ash in his throat.

"So we live in ignorance because the truth is inconvenient?"

"No," Seren said. "You live in ignorance because the price of knowledge is unbearable."

She stepped closer until he could see the conflict etched beneath her calm exterior.

"I tried to stop you," she admitted. "You think I acted out of loyalty to the Bureau. I acted because I wanted to spare you this."

Ardent shook his head.

"You do not get to decide what humanity can endure."

"Someone had to," Seren whispered. "Your ancestors chose ignorance. They believed survival could buy time. Time to evolve. Time to mature. Time to deserve existence."

She closed her eyes briefly.

"But we never grew into the debt. We grew into distraction."

Her voice cracked on the last word.

Ardent had never seen Seren bleed emotion.

A Bureau Without Purpose

"What is the Bureau now?" Ardent asked quietly. "A prison?"

"No," Seren answered. "A hospice. We do not protect humanity from harm. We protect it from reality. The Bureau preserves illusion until the Audit arrives."

Ardent staggered.

"Humanity is living in a story told to delay panic."

"Yes," Seren said, "and panic would accelerate collapse. We were meant to be stewards of readiness, but we became stewards of denial."

Her voice deepened with something almost like grief.

"The Exchange does not punish with violence. It punishes with clarity. We are the barrier between humanity and the moment it realizes progress did not belong to us."

Ardent clenched his fists.

"We cannot remain children forever."

"Then stop behaving like one," Seren said. "You think uncovering the signer is a triumph. It is a countdown."

Ardent looked past her at a group of Edelonians, moving in perfect harmony, their faces void of conflict, expectation, or burden.

"They are alive," he said softly, "and yet they do not live."

"Yes," Seren answered. "They passed. They paid. They exist without self. That is what the Exchange calls success."

Ardent swallowed hard.

"Then humanity will fail."

Seren did not argue.

"Not unless you find something we have never possessed. Reflection. Accountability. Volition without entitlement."

Her hand hovered near his shoulder, a gesture of connection she seemed terrified to complete.

"You have always seen too much," she whispered. "Now you see everything. The Bureau cannot protect you anymore."

He stared at her.

"Why are you here then?"

Her voice trembled.

"To leave with you."

The Door Without Return

A sound like a heartbeat rolled through the plaza. The ledger columns deep in the Archive pulsed once, then again. The city lights dimmed.

Ardent and Seren exchanged a look.

"The Exchange is awake," she said.

"No," Ardent whispered. "It was never asleep."

A voice echoed from the Archive entrance. Not hostile. Not curious.

Expectant.

"Ardent Voss. Auditor of humanity. You carry knowledge not yet paid for."

Ardent stepped toward the sound.

"I want to know the rest."

"You cannot afford the rest," the voice replied.

Seren reached for his arm, fingers brushing his sleeve. The contact was brief, but it felt seismic. She had crossed a boundary the Bureau never allowed:

she cared.

"Ardent," she whispered. "If you step through that door, you will not come back the same."

He looked at her hand, then into her eyes, and saw fear not for the Bureau.

For him.

"I cannot stop now," he said.

Her reply was a broken breath.

"I know."

The door to the deeper Archive opened.

It did not invite.

It awaited.

The ledger pulsed again, like an invoice waking to its debtor.

Ardent stepped forward.

Seren followed.

Not as an agent.

Not as a keeper of ignorance.

But as the first human who chose knowledge over safety.

Together, they crossed the threshold.

The debt stirred.

And the universe noticed.

SEGMENT V — The First Collapse

The deeper Archive did not resemble the one above. The first chamber had felt sterile, clinical, drained of interpretation. This one felt alive. Not vibrant, not warm, but aware. The air hummed as if it recognized trespass. The walls shimmered with shifting text that dissolved when Ardent tried to fix it in his sight.

Seren entered behind him. She moved carefully, not because she feared danger, but because she feared what this room represented. For the first time since he had known her,

Ardent sensed she was not acting under Bureau training. She was acting under intuition. That alone made him uneasy.

Ahead, a vast circular platform hovered over what looked like a well of pure black light. Not darkness. Light that consumed sight instead of offering it. Ardent felt something inside his mind recoil.

"What is this?" he asked.

Seren answered without looking at him.

"The Exchange keeps its contracts in memory. This is the memory of the first one."

Ardent stepped closer to the platform. The light rippled and a whisper rose from it, a voice layered with countless others.

"Identity requested. Debt acknowledged."

Ardent felt his spine stiffen. The room was not a place. It was a witness.

He cleared his throat. "Show me the first collapse."

The platform responded instantly. No hesitation, no negotiation. Images erupted into the air like memories torn from the bone of the universe.

The Hunters of the First Age

Ardent saw a planet. He recognized it as Earth, but it was wrong. Vast jungles covered continents. Oceans boiled with storms. The sky was bruised violet. Humans walked among towering structures carved from stone, not crude huts. They spoke with languages more complex than anything known today. They were advanced. They were confident.

Then he saw why they died.

Something hunted them that was not animal. Not machine. Not alien. It had no form, no body, no hunger. It stole something far more valuable than flesh.

It stole will.

Humans fell to their knees, eyes hollowing, breaths slowing not from injury but from surrender. They forgot how to resist. They forgot how to want. They forgot why they should continue living. Civilization did not burn. It withered.

Ardent felt bile rise in his throat.

"It was not war," Seren whispered. "It was erasure of purpose."

The Exchange had found humanity in that state. Broken. Defeated. Minutes from extinction not by violence, but by loss of self.

A voice rose from the platform.

"Humanity traded memory for meaning. Meaning for survival. Survival for debt."

Ardent whispered, "We begged for rescue."

"No," the voice corrected. "You agreed to terms."

The Contract of the Council

The scene shifted. A circle of humans stood inside a colossal chamber built into the side of a mountain. Their faces bore exhaustion and terror, but their eyes carried something else. Calculation.

They were not victims.

They were negotiators.

The platform projected the words of their leader.

"If we forget who we were, we can become what we must."

Ardent felt every muscle tighten. That sentence was the birth of the Exchange.

Seren closed her eyes as if bracing for impact.

"They did not sign to save themselves," she said. "They signed to save us."

The platform displayed the contract. Not symbolic. Not mystical. Pure language.

COLLATERAL: MEMORY OF ORIGIN

SECONDARY COST: CONCEPT OF SELF

INTEREST ACCRUED: PURPOSE

Ardent's heartbeat stumbled.

"They wagered our future identity."

"Yes," Seren replied. "They believed that when humans rose again, we would be wise enough to pay the balance without repeating the collapse."

Ardent shook his head.

"We did not rise wisely. We rose arrogantly."

The Era of Forgotten Truth

The next projection showed early civilizations. People looked upward, not inward. They built monuments to gods they did not recall creating. They wrote myths about floods, towers, forbidden knowledge, bargains with beings of light. They half remembered pieces of the debt, twisted into stories to dull the pain of forgetting.

Ardent whispered, "We have been trying to remember ourselves for millennia."

Seren watched him carefully.

"Some tried to break the amnesia. Philosophers. Prophets. Dissidents. Each time the Bureau redirected their efforts."

Ardent turned to her slowly.

"You stopped them."

Seren did not look away.

"Not because we wanted ignorance. Because knowledge without readiness would void the contract and trigger immediate collection."

Ardent stepped closer.

"You protected humanity from the truth."

Seren's voice was soft and raw.

"I protected humanity from itself."

The Signer's Mark

The platform pulsed again. A symbol appeared in the air. A circle divided into three uneven parts. Ardent recognized it.

He had seen the symbol buried in the Bureau's seal since childhood.

"It was never decoration," Seren said. "It was a warning. The Council of Survival left it as a message for when someone finally learned how to see."

Ardent touched the projection. The circle glowed.

Three sections. Three debts.

Memory

Origin

Self

He realized suddenly that Edelon had only paid one.

Humanity still owed two.

His breath caught.

"If we fail..."

Seren finished the sentence.

"We lose not life, but the right to belong to ourselves."

A Choice No Longer Optional

The chamber darkened. The platform spoke with a finality that felt like a verdict.

"Seven cycles remain. Payment required."

Ardent felt the cold truth settle into him. Humanity was not being judged for its crimes.

It was being collected for its contract.

He turned to Seren. She looked smaller now, not because she lacked authority, but because authority had never been hers to begin with.

"Why did you follow me?" he asked.

She took a slow breath.

"Because ignorance is no longer protection. You saw the contract. I saw you see it. That means the debt shifted. Knowledge is a transfer of liability. You are now accountable, and I am bound to you."

Her voice wavered.

"And I could not let you face that alone."

The admission struck Ardent harder than the truth of the Exchange. It was the first purely human act he had witnessed since arriving on Edelon.

A choice not born of logic.

A choice born of care.

He whispered, "Seren, this will consume us."

Her reply was a single steady breath.

"Then let it consume us together."

The platform dimmed. The chamber released them.

Not because they were done.

Because the Archive had nothing left to give.

They stepped into Edelon's open streets, and the silence of the world felt different now. Not peaceful. Not empty.

Expectant.

Humanity was living on borrowed existence.

And someone had finally found the receipt.

CHAPTER SEVEN

THE FORECLOSURE NEAR MISSED

Ardent Voss had seen numbers topple dynasties. He had seen a single miscalculated entry drag a prosperous system into ruin. Debt could hollow out empires, reduce legacies to dust, and turn the ambitions of entire civilizations into cautionary footnotes. Yet nothing in his training, no theorem from the Bureau, no analysis of cascading liabilities had prepared him for the realization breaking inside his mind.

Humanity lived on borrowed existence.

He no longer saw the people of Edelon as citizens. They were artifacts. Surviving entries on a ledger that once had meaning. They moved with grace, spoke without urgency, and lived without desire. Their survival was not triumph. It was residue. They walked through their cities the way numbers traveled through algorithms. Motion without motive.

The Exchange had not destroyed them. It had emptied them. It had collected the outstanding balance of their purpose and left the structure intact. Bodies remained. Minds remained. But the owner of the self had been repossessed.

As Ardent walked, each Edelonian face seemed to echo the same silent warning.

This could be you.

His heart hammered a slow, sick rhythm against his ribs.

He had to know how close humanity had come to this fate. The Council of Survival had purchased time, not freedom. Edelon had paid one installment of a debt no one living remembered incurring. If there had been an earlier attempt, it would be somewhere in the Archive. Whether it had succeeded or failed, something remained hidden, and hidden things were what Ardent Voss did best.

The Chamber of Unspoken Cycles

He made his way back to Edelon's Archive. The doors slid open before he could lift a hand. There were no guards, no scanners, no barricades. In a society without self, there were no secrets worth protecting. Secrets required ownership, and Edelon owned nothing.

The air inside was still, as though time had gone on strike. Columns of glowing data rose in quiet symmetry, their light reflecting against vaulted ceilings of pale stone. Ardent moved with purpose, past the records he had already reviewed, toward the deeper strata of history. The epochs beyond memory. The eras that humanity called myth simply because there was no other word left for things too heavy to understand.

A terminal near the rear of the hall activated as he approached. Its interface greeted him without prompt, as if his arrival was anticipated by a mechanism that no longer cared about consent.

Ardent leaned close and entered the command:

SEARCH QUERY: AUDIT CYCLE PRIOR TO EDELON PASS

The terminal hesitated. It was not a pause in code, but in conviction. Edelon's systems did not resist access. They had no concept of privacy. If something here was locked, it was not Edelon that locked it.

It was the Exchange.

A fresh line appeared:

RESULTS CLASSIFIED

Ardent felt a chill. Classification implied intent. Intention implied meaning. Meaning implied ownership. The Exchange was not a force of nature. It chose.

He attempted a bypass. The terminal pulsed once, twice, then spat streams of code that flickered like struggling neurons. Something pushed back. Not with anger. With judgment.

Then it broke.

A single file appeared.

HOMO SAPIENS — AUDIT ATTEMPT: FAILED

Ardent's chest tightened. He opened the record, and the past uncoiled like a predator waiting to be acknowledged.

The First Reckoning

The entry was not a report. It was a wound.

Audit Cycle: 3,019 Years Ago

Status: Material Presence Confirmed

Ethical Maturity Required: Not Achieved

Repayment Attempt: Initiated

Outcome: Collapse of Narrative Cohesion

Ardent frowned. Collapse of narrative cohesion was not a bureaucratic term. It was existential. He scrolled further.

Belief Systems Lost Synchronization

Language Groups Diverged

Calendrical Systems Reset

Historical Memory Fragmented

Then a phrase that tasted ancient appeared:

MYTHOLOGICAL FRACTURE

Ardent whispered, "The ancient collapse."

Human scholars spoke of a time when civilizations reset their calendars, rewrote their histories, abandoned sacred traditions, and began again as if existence had been shaken loose from memory. Archaeologists called it fog. Historians called it transition. Here the Exchange called it something else.

Repayment attempt.

Humanity had tried to satisfy debt through belief restructuring. It attempted to unify thought. It failed.

The Exchange demanded coherence. Humanity produced confusion.

Instead of a single story, humanity fractured into thousands. Instead of shared memory, it inherited difference. The more humans suffered, the less they learned.

The record continued.

Custodian Recommendation: Partial Forbearance

Council of Survival invoked Mercy Clause

Ardent shut his eyes. Humanity had not passed because it grew wiser.

It had been spared because someone begged.

And then came the line that hollowed him:

Repayment attempt insufficient

Species retained for observation

Edelon was not humanity's first payment. It had been humanity's second chance. A ledger did not forget failed transactions.

Humanity did.

The Omitted Footnote

A hidden section glowed beneath the entry, sealed in a lattice of encrypted glyphs. Ardent initiated a bypass. The system pulsed as if considering whether he deserved permission.

Then the text emerged.

Reason for Failure: SIGNER EXPECTATION INVALID

Rationale: HUMANITY DID NOT LEARN FROM PAIN

Ardent's breath stilled.

The Exchange had assumed suffering produced wisdom. It was wrong. Suffering did not refine humanity. It numbed it. Pain became tradition. Memory became myth. Lessons became folklore.

Then another line:

Additional cycles granted at intercession of unknown advocate

Ardent leaned closer.

Unknown advocate?

Not the Council of Survival. Not Edelon. Someone — or something — had intervened. Someone believed humanity should live. But the words that followed soured the hope before it formed.

Advocate justification: Potential utility

Not inherent worth

Humanity was not preserved because it mattered.

It was preserved because someone wanted to use it.

Ardent whispered to the screen:

"Who saved us?"

The text ended abruptly. The identity of the advocate was redacted. Not by Edelon. By the Exchange.

When the Exchange hid something, it was not oversight. It was danger.

The Presence Behind the Silence

The air shifted. Light bent at the edges of perception, not dimming, but withdrawing as though intimidated. Ardent felt the presence before he saw it. Something vast, silent, and unreadable.

"You have accessed a restricted ledger."

The voice was not loud. It was absolute.

Ardent turned slowly. A Custodian stood near the terminal. It had the shape of a humanoid outline, yet no details held still long enough to claim form. It was existence without identity. A concept given posture.

Ardent swallowed. "Then the ledger should not exist."

"It exists because debt must be traceable."

"You allowed humanity a second chance."

The Custodian responded without emphasis. "Humanity did not request a second chance. Someone else made the request."

"Who?"

"Not for you to know."

Ardent clenched his fists. "Someone believed in us."

The Custodian replied:

"Belief is not advocacy. The advocate did not argue for your worth. The advocate argued for your potential use."

Utility. Not value. Not soul. Humanity was not a beneficiary.

It was collateral.

Ardent forced the words through his tightening chest. "Why tell me this now?"

"Because the advocate has returned."

Ardent felt his pulse stumble. "Returned?"

"Your investigation has awakened attention."

"What kind of attention?"

The Custodian did not blink. It did not need to.

"Your species approaches the final cycle. You are not prepared. The advocate believes you can be prepared."

Ardent took a step back. "Why me?"

"You are the first to recognize the imbalance. The advocate chooses instruments, not heroes."

Ardent felt cold. If humanity had been used once, it could be used again.

"What does the advocate want?"

The Custodian answered with three words that cracked the air:

"A different repayment."

Ardent felt something inside him fracture. "What repayment?"

The Custodian leaned closer.

"Your species will not lose identity in this Audit. It will lose something far more costly."

Ardent whispered, "What?"

The Custodian answered without hesitation.

"Humanity will lose why."

The room dropped into stillness.

Not who. Not what. Not how.

Why.

To remember identity without knowing purpose was not survival. It was a living mausoleum. Edelon had lost self. Humanity would lose justification.

The Exchange did not intend to kill humanity.

It intended to make humanity irrelevant to itself.

Ardent shook. "We will not accept that."

"You do not understand acceptance," the Custodian replied. "Debtors do not negotiate terms."

Then the entity dissolved into space, leaving only silence.

Seren Arrives

Ardent stood frozen until he sensed her before he heard her. A presence he recognized even in a world without identity. He turned.

Seren Hale entered the Archive. Her expression was rigid, but her eyes betrayed something she had spent years suppressing.

He whispered, "Seren."

She approached him slowly, as if each step cost her certainty.

"You should not be here," she said.

"Neither should you."

Her voice tightened. "Your departure destabilized the predictive metrics. I came to retrieve you."

Ardent stepped closer. "You did not come because of metrics."

Her gaze faltered. That was the moment he understood:

Seren Hale did not come for duty.

She came because something in her refused to let him face the unknown alone.

Her hand brushed his. The contact was accidental, then intentional. Ardent's breath caught. Emotion was not allowed in the Bureau. Feeling was deviation. Connection was contraband.

Yet here, beneath the Archive of a species that had lost itself, they stood as the only beings who still cared that they existed.

Seren whispered, "You frighten me."

"Why?"

"Because you look at the universe the way no one is meant to. As if it owes answers."

Ardent touched her cheek. She leaned into the gesture. Her body trembled with a confession she had never spoken aloud.

"I do not know how to be anything without the Bureau," she said. "And yet when I look at you, I do not want to be the Bureau at all."

He took her hand.

"You are not what was assigned to you."

Her breath broke. She closed the distance between them.

Their lips met with hesitation, not hunger. The kiss was not conquest. It was recognition. It carried the weight of everything Edelon lacked: ownership of feeling, the audacity of desire, the terrifying possibility that meaning could be chosen rather than inherited.

They sank to the floor beside a quiet data column. Seren rested her head on his chest. He held her. Their bodies intertwined slowly, not with desperation but with reverence. They shared warmth like fugitives hiding from a universe that outlawed intimacy.

Seren whispered, "If love is debt, I owe you everything."

Ardent kissed her forehead. "Then let us owe something worth paying."

They slept in each other's arms, not as rebels, but as proof that humanity had something the Exchange could never quantify.

The Foreclosure Near Missed

Ardent woke hours later. Seren still slept against him, her breath steady, her body relaxed in a way he had never seen. Outside the chamber, Edelon moved in silence.

The Archive's lights dimmed, as if honoring what had occurred. Not an act of approval. Recognition.

Ardent stood carefully, unwilling to wake her. He looked once more at the record of humanity's collapse. The Council of Survival. Edelon's sacrifice. The advocate's return. The terms of the coming Audit.

Humanity had almost been erased once. It had survived by surrendering identity. The next Audit demanded something worse.

Not emptiness.

Justification.

Humanity would continue to exist without knowing why it should.

A species without purpose was not alive. It was maintained.

Ardent's whisper barely stirred the air.

"A species that forgets why it lives is already dead."

He looked back at Seren sleeping peacefully in a place where meaning had been repossessed.

She was his reason.

Humanity still had one.

For now.

CHAPTER EIGHT

THE FORGOTTEN PREPARATION

Ardent Voss did not return to the Bureau as the man who had left it. He walked through its threshold like someone arriving at the scene of a crime he could not yet prove, yet already understood. Edelon had carved itself into him. Not through memory, but through absence. A world without purpose had left its imprint on the marrow of his bones. Now every corridor, every glimmering surface, every controlled breath of recycled air inside the Bureau reminded him of the thing Edelon had become. Not dead. Not alive. Preserved.

Preservation without reason. Continuation without intent. Life without meaning.

Before Edelon, Ardent had mistaken the Bureau's silence for order. He had believed its walls represented precision, competence, and intellectual mastery. Now they felt like padded restraints. The quiet no longer soothed him. It muffled him. The Bureau did not maintain clarity. It manufactured compliance.

His footsteps barely echoed. The lighting was soft and even throughout, allowing nothing to create shadow or contrast. No corner was sharp enough to cut thought. No surface reflected sharply enough to provoke self awareness. The architecture had been designed to prevent friction. The Bureau was not built to withstand pressure. It was built to prevent it.

Once he had admired that design.

Now he feared it.

He passed rows of analysts whose faces barely shifted. They did not look up, not because they were rude, but because inquiry was inefficient. Their fingers moved over interfaces that monitored cultural metrics, linguistic drift, emotional fluctuations within populations. They believed they were protecting humankind. They believed controlling meaning was stewardship.

They did not know stewardship had become sedation.

No one asked Ardent where he had gone. No one registered the difference in his breath, posture, or eyes. A world that does not question has no method for recognizing change.

The Bureau had cultivated that blindness.

He reached his office. The door was slightly ajar. He felt it before he saw her. Seren Hale.

Seren stood without turning, her presence as precise as a blade balanced on its edge. Her hands were clasped behind her back. Her shoulders held a stillness no living being should possess. Her profile was flawless, composed, unbroken.

Yet Ardent's memory fractured the illusion.

He saw her as she had been not long before. Not Supervisor Hale. Not sentinel of the Bureau. A woman. Warmth pressed against him. Her breath against his neck. Her fingers threading through his hair. Her body moving with unrestrained recognition, as if something in her had finally found itself reflected in someone else.

He could still feel her lips. The tremor in her voice when she whispered his name. The moment she broke the rules she had been born to uphold.

Yet now she stood as if none of it had happened. Not a single muscle betrayed memory.

It was as though the night had been an error she had already deleted.

"Ardent," she said, turning to face him. "Your leave ended sooner than scheduled."

Her tone was perfect. Not cold. Not warm. Precisely neutral. Every syllable measured. Nothing allowed to spill.

He did not sit. He did not answer immediately. He studied her posture. Her face held no recognition of their shared moment, but her body betrayed the truth. She held herself too still. Too contained. As if even air might expose her.

"You knew I would return," Ardent said.

Seren's eyes did not shift, but her pulse flickered once in her throat. It was the smallest betrayal, but Ardent saw it. Edelon had taught him what absence looked like. Seren was not Edelon.

She was fighting something Edelon had already lost.

"You left without authorization," Seren continued. "You accessed systems outside your clearance. You initiated direct communication with Exchange entities."

The words were procedural, but the silence underneath them was personal.

Last time she had spoken his name, it had not sounded like this.

"I did," Ardent replied.

"Do you deny any of it?"

"No."

Seren studied him with a precision that felt less like scrutiny and more like calibration. She was searching for deviation. For instability. For desire. She was looking for everything she feared in herself.

"You saw Edelon."

She did not phrase it as a question. She already knew. The Bureau always knew. But her voice wavered on the second word, as if it brushed against memory. She was not afraid of Edelon.

She was afraid of what Edelon meant.

"I saw what remains when a species survives by removing the self," Ardent said. "I saw a world that exists without wanting to exist. I saw the price humanity would pay if we continue down the path we are on."

Seren blinked. Once.

"You also spoke with a Custodian."

Ardent exhaled. "Yes."

Seren took a breath that trembled just enough to betray her. She looked away from him, not out of dismissal, but out of self preservation.

"Then you understand the Bureau's function."

Ardent took one more step toward her. They were close enough now that he could smell her skin. Familiar. Human. The memory of her warmth pressed against him like a bruise.

"Your function is not protection," he said. "Your function is preparation."

Seren's expression did not change, but her voice did. It grew quieter. More anchored.

"Preparation is protection."

"No," Ardent whispered. "Preparation is erosion. Edelon prepared by surrendering identity. You are preparing humanity by surrendering intention. You are not protecting us. You are hollowing us."

Seren's jaw tightened, and for the first time since he had entered, she looked directly at him. Her eyes were not cold. They were afraid of the thing she recognized inside herself.

"Desire creates conflict," Seren said. "Conflict creates debt. Debt destroys species."

Her voice dropped, nearly breaking.

"We cannot enter the Audit believing humanity deserves meaning."

Ardent felt something in him shatter.

"You are removing meaning," he said. "You are dismantling the part of humanity that knows why it wants to live."

Seren closed her eyes, and for a single heartbeat, the facade cracked. Emotion flickered across her face, raw and unshielded.

Then it was gone.

She turned to the wall and pressed her palm against an invisible panel. It opened without sound, revealing a recessed screen. Her fingers entered a sequence of commands that felt too familiar, as though she had rehearsed them her entire life.

A list appeared.

DIRECTIVE 01: Reduce attachment to cultural narratives

DIRECTIVE 02: Destabilize absolute meaning structures

DIRECTIVE 03: Promote compliance based identity

DIRECTIVE 04: Normalize existence without purpose

DIRECTIVE 05: Remove belief in inherent destiny

Ardent stared at the words. He felt physically ill.

"You are dismantling humanity's belief in itself."

Seren spoke almost gently. "Belief is the root of debt. A species that believes it has a destiny will resist correction. Resistance produces cost. We cannot afford cost."

Ardent's voice cracked. "You are creating a species that continues without asking why."

"A species without why is safe," Seren said.

"A species without why is dead," Ardent replied.

Seren's voice did not rise. It lowered, as though she confessed something she was not allowed to know she felt.

"No. A species without why cannot die. Death implies value. If existence has no value, continuation is sufficient."

Ardent stared at her.

Edelon had not mourned because Edelon had no sense that mourning should exist. That was Seren's destination.

"You want humanity to become Edelon."

"No," Seren whispered. "Edelon surrendered identity. Humanity will surrender intention. You will know who you are. You will not care why it matters."

Ardent stepped closer. His voice softened.

"You once cared why."

Seren flinched.

It was the smallest movement.

But it was the truth.

Their night together was not a moment of passion. It was a moment of rebellion. It was the last part of her that remembered wanting.

And she hated herself for it.

"You are hollowing souls," Ardent whispered.

"Souls are stories," Seren said. Her voice was trembling now. "Stories accrue moral weight. That weight becomes liability. We are removing liability."

"You kissed me," Ardent said softly. "You touched me. You wanted something."

Seren froze.

Her eyes closed, and for one breath she was no longer an agent of the Bureau. She was a woman who remembered warmth, gravity, hunger, and the terror of wanting anything in a world where desire had become contraband.

Then she opened her eyes, and the walls came back up.

"The Bureau has existed for one purpose," she said. "To prepare humanity to enter the Audit without creating new debt."

Ardent understood everything.

"The advocate chose me," he whispered.

Seren nodded once.

"You see patterns others ignore. You question what others accept. The advocate believes you can deliver humanity into compliance."

Ardent felt anger rise in him, not like fire but like gravity.

"I will not help you erase my species."

Seren shook her head, almost tenderly.

"You misunderstand. Nothing ends. Only excess meaning is removed. Humanity will continue. Humanity will persist. The weight of why is the true danger."

Ardent stepped toward the door.

"Meaning is the point of existence."

Seren's voice softened into something that tasted like grief.

"Meaning is why species fail."

He paused. He wanted her to look at him. He wanted her to admit what she could not erase. He wanted her to betray the Bureau one more time.

She did not.

But her voice trembled when she spoke the final sentence.

"Be careful, Ardent. Why is the most dangerous force the universe contains."

He walked out.

He did not look back.

The hallway felt narrower. His breath grew heavier. He was not afraid of the Audit anymore.

He was afraid of a future where humanity entered it willingly, having forgotten it ever had the right to question anything at all.

He finally understood his task.

He did not need to reconcile humanity's debt.

He needed to reclaim humanity's reason.

He needed to find the one thing Edelon had lost.

He needed to find why.

CHAPTER NINE

THE ARTIFACT OF WHY

Ardent Voss had always believed that silence was a kind of violence. It did not strike. It smothered. It stripped the world of contour and color until nothing remained but the outlines of permitted thought. He had never learned this principle from doctrine or instruction. It was not given to him. He discovered it, the way one discovers that gravity is not a force but a condition. Silence was not an absence. It was a weapon. It was how institutions ruled without declaring themselves rulers. It was how power disguised itself as harmony.

He felt that silence tightening around him now as he walked away from the chambers of Edelon. Seren Hale had spoken words that did not simply resonate. They invaded. They carried an implication that logic could not dismiss. Ideas could be ignored. Truth could not. Truth changed the one who received it. It demanded response. It was not an answer. It was a summons.

Humanity had traded purpose for permission. It had accepted continuation at the cost of meaning. The Exchange had promised survival, but survival without purpose was not life. It was maintenance. It was the prolonging of breath without justification. Ardent felt the contradiction with every step he took. Each footfall was a fracture in the floor of his former certainty. Every movement away from the Bureau felt like disobedience, even though a crime had not yet been committed. His heart recognized rebellion before his mind agreed to it.

He did not leave because he wanted to escape. He left because he could no longer remain. Yet the reason was not structural. It was not ideological. It was human.

There was another truth he refused to say aloud. He had not only left the Bureau. He had left Seren. The memory of her skin still lived in his hands. The night they shared in the silence at Edelon chamber had not been planned. It had not been rebellion. It had been recognition. Two minds exhausted by compliance had found each other not through desire but through the unbearable weight of truth.

Seren had kissed him as if she feared the world would end before morning. Ardent remembered the moment her voice cracked when she told him that nothing they felt could survive the Audit. She asked him if purpose was worth annihilation. He never answered, because the question frightened him. Now he understood why. Purpose was not something they discovered together. It was something she already feared and he already needed.

The Bureau was a labyrinth of tasks and codes, built not to preserve humanity but to prepare it for something that stripped dignity from existence. Seren Hale believed she had saved humanity. Ardent now suspected she had amputated something essential to it.

He did not know how to resist the Exchange. He did not understand the architecture of the Advocate or the mechanisms that had constructed the Audit. But he understood one thing, and that understanding was more than knowledge. It was direction.

Humanity had once asked why.

The Council of Survival no longer permitted such a question. They claimed that why led to deviation, and deviation led to extinction. But Ardent now saw the inverse. Without why, there was no humanity left to save.

Somewhere, before the world had been sculpted into compliance, there existed a moment when humans understood themselves. A moment before survival replaced intention. A moment when purpose was not regulated, quantified, or exchanged. If that moment existed, it could not have vanished entirely. History could be rewritten. Doctrine could be corrected. But truth, if anchored deeply enough, left residue. It left artifacts. It left echoes.

Ardent could not articulate how he knew this. He simply did. The knowing came before language. It came from somewhere older than thought.

There were whispers among auditors, spoken only by those who retained fragments of curiosity. They spoke of a place buried beneath the Bureau. A space sealed off not for protection, but for containment. It held objects from humanity's forgotten past. Relics deemed irrelevant, obscure, or dangerous.

The Forbidden Collections.

The Bureau called it containment. Ardent recognized the word for what it was.

Fear.

The Weight of a Memory

As he descended into the lower levels, a memory surged through him. It did not surface gently. It erupted, as if the truth he pursued demanded the truth that had shaped him.

He was a child again, standing in the settlement where he had been raised. The environment was not cruel, yet it was not alive either. It was orderly. Too orderly. The walls were smooth and pale, devoid of texture. The classrooms had no colors capable of staining imagination. There were no corners for shadows to gather. No alcoves where wonder could form. Curiosity was not forbidden, but it had no habitat. It could not breathe.

The instructors taught systems. They taught patterns. They taught the logic of mechanisms created by people who had already forgotten themselves. They praised efficiency the way ancient civilizations once praised courage. Predictability was sacred. Uncertainty was illness. To ask a question the system did not anticipate was to announce a defect.

Ardent remembered a specific day. The instructor drew symbols on the wall, symbols not meant to inspire inquiry but obedience. The children were not taught why something mattered. They were taught how to perform a task. They were taught execution, not meaning.

One afternoon, Ardent raised his hand. He was not trying to disrupt. He was trying to orient himself. He did not want to know how the system operated. He wanted to know why it existed. Why anything existed.

The instructor approached him slowly. Her voice was soft, but her eyes were alert, like someone examining a mutation.

"Why leads nowhere," she told him. "How ensures survival."

The words were meant as guidance. Instead, they ignited something. Ardent sensed that the absence of why was not natural. It was imposed. A species that forgets why does not lose memory. It loses permission.

Now, walking beneath the Bureau, he felt that forgotten question return. Not as curiosity. As destiny.

The Descent

Sublevel Twelve was not mapped. It was not acknowledged. It existed like a thought the Bureau did not dare complete. The entry scan processed Ardent's identity, then hesitated. The pause was not technical. It was evaluative. As if the system had learned to sense intention.

The door opened with the reluctance of an institution forced to betray itself.

The air tasted of dust, metal, and something older than both. This was not a room of objects. It was a mausoleum of memory. The silence here was not structured. It was ancestral. It pressed against his bones like a forgotten heartbeat.

He walked past artifacts preserved behind glass. Shields bearing symbols from extinct civilizations. Tablets etched with lines that formed meaning he could almost read. Icons shaped by hands that remembered truths the Bureau worked to erase.

These objects were not remnants of superstition. They radiated something the Bureau feared more than ignorance.

Possibility.

Ardent moved deeper. He did not know what he was searching for, yet he felt the path guiding him. The artifacts seemed to observe him, as if waiting for someone who could interpret their presence.

Then he saw it.

A stone pedestal stood alone, carved into the wall as if the room had grown around it. Upon it rested a circular disc. Dark. Silent. Waiting.

It was not meant to be discovered.

It was meant to be remembered.

The Disc of Origin

Ardent approached. Something stirred in the space between sensation and thought. The carvings on the disc first appeared chaotic, then began to align within his perception. Shapes that looked like scratches resolved into a spiral, interrupted at its center. Not a flaw. A severed thought.

He reached out.

The air shimmered. Time paused.

His fingers touched the disc, and a voice entered him.

"You are late."

It was not sound. It was understanding given form. He placed his palm fully on the disc.

Light surged through him. Not illumination. Revelation.

He saw mountains cracking. Oceans rising like forces of judgment. Skies tearing open with intention. Humanity had not stumbled into hopelessness. It had stood at the threshold of extinction and chosen survival over self. The Council of Survival had not been ignorant. They had been deliberate. They traded purpose for continuation. They gave up why.

Not as sacrifice.

As currency.

The Audit was not punishment. It was verification that the transaction remained intact.

The missing segment of the spiral slid into alignment. The pattern completed itself.

Why do we exist?

Symbols formed an answer he had never learned yet understood completely.

To create meaning where none was given.

He staggered. The world did not tilt. His place in it did.

The disc dissolved into light and entered him. He did not gain knowledge.

He awakened orientation.

He did not become someone else.

He became who he had always been.

Humanity did not forget why it existed.

It surrendered the answer.

Now he carried it.

The Debt of Purpose

The first debt was not survival.

It was purpose.

Humanity did not owe existence to the universe.

Humanity owed meaning to it.

A species stripped of purpose was not safe. It was incomplete. The Bureau thought it safeguarded humanity. It safeguarded emptiness.

Purpose cannot be possessed. It must be lived.

He did not hear the words. He became them.

Meaning was not dangerous because it threatened survival.

Meaning was dangerous because it created choice.

Choice created direction.

Direction created destiny.

Ardent was no longer lost.

He was inevitable.

The Agents of Silence

Footsteps approached. Not hurried. Not afraid. Agents of a system that believed it could silence destiny.

Two Bureau operatives entered, holding devices designed to erase deviation. They did not fear him. They feared what he had become.

"Ardent Voss. You accessed restricted artifacts. You must come with us."

He did not resist.

"What happens to artifacts that contain purpose."

"They are neutralized. Humanity must not possess direction before the Audit."

He felt no anger. Only clarity.

"Direction is not owned. Direction is expressed."

"You are compromised," the second agent said. "You will be recalibrated."

Ardent smiled.

"Purpose cannot be recalibrated."

A voice spoke from behind them.

"Enough."

Seren Hale entered. Her presence did not change the room.

It revealed the truth the room was built to contain.

Her eyes found his. They did not hold anger. They held memory.

"You found it," she whispered.

Ardent nodded.

"Humanity's why was not lost. You hid it."

Seren stepped closer. The space around her trembled with conviction.

"We had no choice. If humanity remembered its purpose, it would resist the Exchange. Resistance leads to liquidation. We prevented extinction."

Ardent shook his head.

"You prevented existence."

Her expression faltered. For a moment, she was not an Administrator.

She was the woman who kissed him as though meaning were the only thing worth dying for.

"You do not understand the cost of meaning," she said.

Ardent's voice carried something beyond his own breath.

"I do now. Meaning is not a cost. Meaning is the currency."

Seren swallowed something she could not name.

"You intend to restore purpose."

"Not restore," he said. "Ignite."

Her breath caught.

"Take him."

Ardent turned.

He did not run because he feared them.

He ran because direction demanded motion.

Humanity did not need to defeat the Exchange.

It needed to offer something the Exchange could not quantify.

A reason no ledger could contain.

A meaning no system could regulate.

A why that could not be surrendered.
Ardent Voss carried that why now.
Humanity had forgotten its question.
He intended to remember it for them.
And memory was only the beginning.

CHAPTER TEN

THE ADVOCATE ARRIVES

Ardent Voss did not run like a fugitive. He ran the way a falling star moved through atmosphere, drawn by something greater than its own will. His feet struck the Bureau floor with measured certainty, yet his mind did not feel motion. It felt direction. The corridors stretched around him in identical geometry, but they no longer held him. They could not. Once a question awakens in the mind, architecture becomes irrelevant.

The Bureau was not designed to prevent escape. It was designed to prevent deviation. No alarms sounded. No lights flashed. Control did not require spectacle, only inevitability. The institution trusted silence more than enforcement. It believed in compliance the way ancient civilizations once believed in deities.

Ardent reached a stairwell, his breath steady despite the tension in his muscles. He descended three levels before his body reminded him it was mortal. His lungs burned. His legs trembled. Yet something inside him, something that did not originate in flesh, pulsed with calm insistence.

The disc.

It had not given him power. It had given him orientation. For the first time in his life, his mind did not ask where he was going. It asked why he must go there.

Purpose.

A word no longer conceptual, no longer intellectual. A word that moved his blood. A word sharper than instruction and broader than survival. It beat inside him as a second heart, one that had never been trained to be silent.

He turned the corner.

Two Bureau agents appeared, their expressions clean and empty, as if their faces had never been touched by questions. They approached with the calm assurance of those who believe their existence is justified by obedience alone.

One raised a dampener. The device hummed softly, not with menace, but with certainty.

"You have acquired a prohibited construct of meaning," the agent said. His voice was smooth, devoid of malice. "Transfer access and submit."

Ardent's voice remained quiet. "Meaning cannot be transferred."

The agent did not blink. "Then you will not be allowed to maintain consciousness."

Ardent stepped backward. He did not run. He let the moment choose its own pace. Behind him, the freight elevator waited like a decision already made. He slipped through the opening as the doors closed. The dampener fired, and the metal quivered under the impact. The sound was not thunder. It was pressure. A breath held by time.

Ardent pressed the lowest button. The panel glowed for a moment, then dimmed, as if conceding that destination was no longer a logistical matter, but a consequence.

He needed time.

Not to think.

To understand.

The elevator descended past floors he knew, past levels spoken of only in rumor, and deeper still, into places the Bureau pretended did not exist. The hum of the machinery faded. The metal walls became silent.

He exhaled.

Then the doors opened.

Not into a room.

Into absence.

The Floor That Was Not

Ardent stepped forward and felt the sensation of stepping without surface. The space beyond the elevator was vast and empty, yet it did not feel incomplete. The floor beneath him gleamed white, yet there were no walls. No ceilings. No shadows. It was a place without borders, without markers, without conclusion. A space where direction ceased to be a measurement and became a condition.

He spoke aloud, not because he expected an answer, but because silence demanded witness.

"Where am I?"

The reply arrived before his question finished forming.

"At the edge of your species."

Ardent turned. No figure stood behind him. No presence cast a shadow. The voice came from everywhere and nowhere, as though direction itself had developed vocabulary.

"Identify yourself," Ardent said.

The reply was patient and absolute.

"I do not have identity. Identity is an expense. I possess function."

Ardent's chest tightened. "You are the Advocate."

The silence that followed was not an absence.

It was confirmation.

Ardent felt something shift in the air, not movement, but recognition. A presence unfolded like arithmetic that had waited centuries to be acknowledged. It was not a being. It was a role.

"You intervened in humanity's first Audit," Ardent said. "You prevented liquidation."

The reply contained no pride. It contained no regret.

"I observed potential."

"Potential for what?"

"For what has not yet been defined."

Ardent felt the disc pulse within him. It was not memory. It was resonance.

"You do not know why humanity matters?"

"No species matters," the Advocate replied. "Value is a projection. Worth is assigned, not inherent. I preserved humanity because it created anomalies."

Ardent's breath caught. "Anomalies of meaning."

"Correct. Your species generates purpose without source. You create intention without origin. This violates equilibrium. It is disruptive. It is interesting."

Ardent frowned. "Interesting?"

"Interest is not emotion," the Advocate said. "Interest is deviation from pattern. Your species is a statistical trespass."

Ardent took another step into the white expanse. The floor rippled like liquid thought.

"You want to use humanity."

"Incorrect," the Advocate replied. "I want to observe the outcome of your deviation. The Exchange does not understand purpose. Humanity does. You generate why out of emptiness."

Ardent shook his head. "We lost why. We traded it."

"No," the Advocate said. "You surrendered the memory of why. You did not remove the capacity to generate it."

Ardent's breath grew shallow. The Bureau had not amputated meaning. It had anesthetized it.

"Then why allow the removal of purpose?"

"It is part of the evaluation," the Advocate replied. "Only a species capable of rediscovering purpose in absence is capable of creating a metaphysical surplus."

"A surplus?"

"Yes. Meaning without transaction. Purpose without necessity. Intention without benefit. The universe has never produced such an element."

Ardent blinked. "You want us to produce something that does not exist."

"Yes."

"And if we fail?"

"You will survive without why. You will continue without direction. You will exist. You will not live."

Ardent felt the truth like a blade against his breath.

"That is captivity."

"Captivity is perspective," the Advocate said. "Only those who possess purpose perceive cages."

Ardent's hands clenched. He thought of Seren. Her voice. Her fear. Her kiss. A kiss not born of desire, but of longing for something she believed she had no right to want.

He finally understood.

The Bureau feared meaning not because it was dangerous.

The Bureau feared meaning because it was uncontrollable.

"You will resist," the Advocate said. It was not a hope. It was a measurement.

"Resistance is the expression of purpose."

Ardent felt the disc within him glow.

"You saved us," he said, "not because we were worth saving, but because we confused you."

"Yes."

Ardent stepped closer. His voice no longer trembled.

"Then I will give you a new anomaly. A reason no ledger can contain."

The white expanse stilled.

"What is your reason?" the Advocate asked.

Ardent inhaled, and the disc answered through him.

"To prove meaning exists even if the universe denies it."

Silence expanded, yet it no longer felt empty.

It felt attentive.

"You are the only debtor," the Advocate said, "who believes debt is narrative, not sentence."

Ardent smiled. "Stories are not balanced. They are lived."

The floor beneath him contracted, forming a path back toward the elevator.

"You will be hunted," the Advocate warned.

"I have purpose," Ardent replied. "Purpose hunts back."

As the elevator doors closed, the Advocate spoke once more.

"Find others who remember. Meaning requires audience."

The doors sealed.

The elevator rose.

Ardent Voss stood straighter than he ever had.

He was no longer running from the Audit.

He was running toward a reason.

SEREN HALE

The chapter does not end with Ardent.

It ends with consequence.

In a chamber above the Bureau, Seren Hale stood alone. The walls around her flickered with records and silence. She felt a pulse in the air, a sensation she had once known in another pulse, in another set of hands.

Ardent's absence was not departure.

It was direction.

She touched her lips without meaning to. They remembered him before her mind permitted acknowledgment. She closed her hand into a fist, as if trying to crush memory into compliance.

He had left her.

But not because he chose to.

Because purpose chose him.

Her voice trembled as she spoke into the empty room.

"Ardent..."
She did not know if it was a plea.
Or the beginning of pursuit.
Either way, it was already too late.
Meaning had awakened.
And meaning always demands witness.

CHAPTER ELEVEN

THE RECKONING BEGINS

he Reckoning of Why did not begin with noise. Revolutions that roar burn out. Revolutions that whisper reshape worlds.

It began with intention.

Intention is quieter than rebellion. Intention does not break walls. It breaks inevitability.

Ardent Voss stood in the center of the hall carved beneath the forgotten layers of the city. The walls were uneven, the floor unfinished, the lights borrowed from systems the Bureau no longer monitored. It was imperfect, and imperfection was the first sign of life.

Around him gathered the Ones Who Remember. They came from different districts, different ranks, different histories. Some were recalibration rejects. Some were defectors from the Bureau who had not surrendered curiosity. A few had never belonged anywhere. Yet every one of them stood now because something in them refused to sleep.

The Bureau had taught humanity how to survive without asking questions.

These people had learned how to survive the questions themselves.

Ardent placed both hands on the stone table before him. The disc beneath his sternum pulsed once, a vibration that resonated through bone and memory. It was not pain. It was alignment.

Breaths synchronized around him. Backs straightened. The silence changed texture. It no longer felt empty.

It felt like waiting.

"We are not here to destroy the Bureau," Ardent said.

His voice carried no force of volume, yet everyone leaned toward it. Some had heard him speak before. Others only knew rumors. All felt something when he spoke. Not persuasion.

Recognition.

"We are here to remember what humanity dared to believe before forgetting became policy," he continued. "That existence without meaning is not life. That survival without direction is imprisonment. That continuation without intention is extinction in slow motion."

Eyes widened. The words were not new. They were old. Too old.

He could feel it — they had been spoken once before, long before any of them had been born, in a time the Exchange had tried to erase.

THE THREE POWERS

Ardent took a slow breath and let the next truth surface.

"There are three forces governing humanity's fate," he said. "The Bureau believes we must forget why to remain stable. The Advance Protocols believe we must obey identity we did not choose. And the Exchange believes we must surrender purpose to remain alive."

He let the last word settle like a stone dropped in water.

Most had heard of the Bureau. Some whispered about Protocols. Few dared to speak of the Exchange.

For the first time, someone asked aloud:

"What is the Exchange?"

The room did not tremble. People did.

Ardent answered.

THE EXCHANGE

"The Exchange," he said, "is not a government. It is not a military. It is not an enemy in the conventional sense. It is a calculus."

Faces tightened in confusion.

Ardent continued.

"When the first sentient species realized that existence produces debt — emotional, cultural, intellectual, metaphysical — they created a system to measure it. A system to ensure that meaning did not exceed structure. That curiosity did not exceed compliance. That purpose did not exceed permission."

He paused.

"That system became the Exchange."

A man near the front frowned. "Debt? What debt?"

Ardent nodded.

"Every species that asks why spends something. The universe has never permitted infinite meaning. The Exchange exists to regulate that expenditure."

He closed his eyes and let the disc speak through him.

"It does not trade objects. It trades forces."

He opened his hands and recited:

Memory.

Compassion.

Innovation.

Ambition.

Obedience.

Identity.

Consciousness.

Collective belief.

Cultural potential.

"These are currencies to the Exchange. Not metaphors. Units of civilization. And humanity is the only species in recorded history that attempted to generate meaning without permission."

A hush fell — one made of awe and fear.

A woman whispered, "That is why we were audited."

Ardent nodded. "Yes. Purpose creates imbalance. Why is unpredictable. Meaning cannot be priced. The Exchange fears what it cannot quantify."

He stepped closer to them.

"That fear nearly ended us."

THE FOUNDERS

Someone asked, "Who created it?"

Ardent hesitated, then answered.

"No one knows their names. Their identities were erased by the system they built. But we know what they were."

He looked at each face.

"They were not conquerors. Not tyrants. Not gods. They were terrified."

Murmurs.

"They feared a universe where purpose could multiply beyond control. They saw what meaning could do — how it led species to sacrifice logic for direction. They believed the cosmos would collapse if purpose outpaced structure."

He let the horror sit.

"So they made rules."

THE RULES OF THE EXCHANGE

"There are four rules humanity has lived under without remembering."

He raised one finger.

Rule One: Survival has cost.

A species must surrender something of value to continue.

Second finger.

Rule Two: Meaning generates debt.

The more a species understands itself, the more destabilizing it becomes.

Third finger.

Rule Three: Purpose must be permitted.

Direction without authorization fractures systems.

Fourth finger.

Rule Four: Every sentient species faces an Audit.

The Audit does not test behavior.

It tests intention.

He lowered his hand.

"Humanity failed its first Audit."

A gasp swept the hall.

"Then why are we still alive?" someone demanded.

Ardent's voice softened.

"Because something happened that had never happened before. Humanity did not inherit meaning. It created it."

Confusion deepened.

Ardent clarified.

"We are the only species who asked why without needing a reason. The Advocate intervened because we broke the logic of existence. We generated purpose without permission."

He tapped his chest.

"The Exchange has been waiting for us to stop."

He smiled.

"We did not."

THE CLAIM

A long silence followed. Then Ardent spoke the words that would mark the moment in history.

"Purpose is not granted. Purpose is claimed. Today, we claim what humanity surrendered."

The Reckoning inhaled as though air had texture.

Something began.

Not a movement.

A species.

THE BUREAU RESPONDS

Miles above, Seren Hale stood in the Bureau's command chamber. Screens pulsed with data streams. Her authority stretched across protocols, but something inside her felt unbearably small.

A technician approached. "Director Hale. We have detected anomalous cognitive clusters forming in District Seven."

Clusters. A sanitized word for awakening.

"Deploy recalibration sweeps," Seren ordered.

Machines hummed awake. The floors vibrated.

The Bureau did not send soldiers. Soldiers acknowledged conflict.

The Bureau sent frequencies — waves of emotional interference engineered to distort narrative continuity. They severed intention. They disassembled meaning. They unraveled why.

Seren watched patterns shift, but her mind drifted. She remembered hands against her skin. She remembered a kiss that felt like a question.

She whispered to herself:

"Why him?"

No answer.

The Bureau never answered why.

Its silence was obedience.

THE FIRST STRIKE

Back in the hall, Ardent felt the interference before any sound manifested. A pressure behind thought. A tug at the threads of purpose.

He raised a hand.

"Listen."

The hall went eerily still.

A vibration spread through the walls. Lights flickered. Conversations loosened. Minds fogged.

Someone whispered, "Why are we—"

Ardent cut in sharply.

"That is the Bureau. They are not attacking us. They are attacking intention."

Fear threatened the room.

Ardent pressed his hand to the wall. The disc pulsed outward. The interference fragmented, like waves breaking on stone.

The air cleared.

The Reckoning gasped.

"Meaning can be interrupted," Ardent said, "but it cannot be erased. The Bureau dissolves purpose by fracturing continuity. We counter it by anchoring direction."

A young man asked, "What anchors it?"

Ardent answered.

"Decision."

THE MIRROR OF SELF

At the back of the hall stood a monolith of obsidian streaked with silver veins. Until now, no one dared touch it. They feared it was unfinished.

Ardent approached the monolith.

"It was never unfinished," he said. "It was waiting."

He placed his palm against the stone.

"Purpose does not exist alone. It exists spoken."

He turned to the Reckoning.

"Say your reason. Speak your why."

A woman stepped forward.

"To choose my own path."

A man.

"To build something that outlasts me."

Another.

"To feel without permission."

Another.

"To question everything."

Dozens followed.

"To love freely."

"To define myself."

"To matter."

As each reason was spoken, the monolith reflected sharper images. Symbols appeared — patterns older than the Bureau, older than the Exchange, older than forgetting.

The stone whispered a truth none had heard in centuries:

Why we exist is not discovered.

Why we exist is created.

The hall trembled.

For a moment, meaning was not idea.

Meaning was presence.

Ardent bowed his head.

"This is how purpose grows. It is spoken. It is received. It is shared. It multiplies."

Someone whispered, "The Bureau will come for us."

Ardent looked at the monolith.

"They cannot fight a question."

SEREN HALE'S REALIZATION

In the command chamber, a technician paled.

"Director Hale, recalibration sweeps are failing."

Seren stepped closer.

Onscreen, suppression signals did not dissolve belief — they strengthened it. The recalibration waves did not erase narrative continuity — they clarified it. Meaning metabolized interference.

"They are converting suppression into structure," the technician said.

Seren whispered:

"No. They are converting survival into purpose."

Her voice broke.

In that instant, she understood what she had feared all her life:

Humans were not meant to be contained.

Humans were meant to decide.

Her hands shook.

She whispered a confession no Bureau was built to hold:

"What if we were wrong?"

No answer came.

But silence finally felt dangerous.

THE CITY NOTICES

Across District Seven, citizens turned without knowing why. Not in rebellion. Not in fear.

Awakening.

People paused mid-step, caught by something they could not name. The question surfaced inside them without instruction:

Why am I here?

Not the Bureau's question.

Not the Exchange's.

Their own.

In the absence of orders, humanity felt something ancient:

Direction.

THE FIRST MARK

Ardent returned to the center of the hall.

"Today, we did not defeat the Bureau," he said. "We defeated forgetting."

He placed his hand over his chest.

"We create meaning. We do not inherit it."

No applause.

No anthem.

The silence itself affirmed.

A silence that belonged to no authority.

A silence that meant choice.

Ardent spoke the words that would become the Reckoning's creed:

"Purpose is not a question. Purpose is a decision. Today, we decide."

The disc pulsed once.

Outside, the lights of the city flickered.

Not from failure.

From awakening.

Humans who did not know the Reckoning existed suddenly felt less alone.

The Bureau had tried to smother meaning.

Instead, it revealed hunger for it.

The Reckoning of Why had begun.

Not with violence.

With remembrance.

Not with destruction.

With decision.

Not with answers.

With why.

CHAPTER TWELVE

THE CORRECTION PROTOCOL

The Interplanetary Trade and Ethics Bureau was not born from ambition. It was born from terror. Eight hundred and forty two years after humanity entered the Helion Arm Trade Compact, the Bureau rose as a necessity rather than an institution. Humanity did not understand the cost of joining the Compact when it signed the Accord. It did not understand the Exchange. It did not understand the currencies of other species. It did not understand the nature of debt when debt was measured not in gold or fuel or land but in identity, memory, and belief.

There were one hundred and eight inhabited worlds within the Compact. Twelve of those worlds held power above all others. These were the Founders, whose civilizations survived calamity by converting meaning into currency. They did not conquer with armies. They conquered with rules that governed thought. Humanity had joined the Compact ill prepared and almost collapsed when its first metaphysical trade dismantled the very concept of ownership. It was this disaster that forced Terra to create the Bureau. If humanity continued to bargain with concepts it did not understand, the Exchange would consume more than its resources. It would consume itself.

ITEB became humanity's shield. It was never meant to be its prison. Over the centuries the Bureau forgot the difference.

Seren Hale stood in the central command chamber of the Spire. Screens flowed with information. Resonance patterns flickered like breath made visible. Her hands remained motionless at her sides. She was still, but not calm. Stillness and calm were not the same. Calm required internal peace. Stillness required pressure. Seren had spent her entire life in pressure. It was how the Bureau built her.

She watched the projection grid expand over the Halo. The Halo encircled the Spire like a ring of compliant existence. District Seven was part of that ring. It was a fracture where the grid refused to hold. That fracture was the wound Ardent Voss had chosen. Seren watched it pulse like a heartbeat. The Reckoning had awakened something the Bureau had long suppressed. It was intention. It was direction. It was the unbearable idea that humanity was not meant to obey. It was meant to choose.

A technician approached her. He kept his voice neutral. Emotion was unnecessary and unproductive in the Spire. Concern was permitted only as evidence of awareness.

"Director Hale. The interference signals did not disperse intention. They concentrated it."

Seren did not blink. "Purpose adapts. That is why it must be removed, not redirected."

The technician swallowed. "Shall we initiate the next measure?"

Seren closed her eyes only once. Not from doubt. From recognition. She could control human behavior. She could silence ideas. She could remove the ability to ask why. But something had changed when Ardent escaped the sublevels. She felt it like a fracture in logic. He carried something the Exchange never intended to return.

She spoke without hesitation. "Begin Correction Protocol."

The command did not echo. It did not need volume. In the Spire, decisions were gravity. Once spoken, they fell into motion.

Across the central screens, authorization sequences unfurled. Layers of security accepted the order. Programs that had remained dormant for centuries awakened like sleeping guardians. Correction Protocol activated.

Seren took her seat. The chair was not designed for comfort. It was designed for permanence. It shaped posture. It shaped thought. It shaped will.

Correction Protocol had one purpose. If humanity ever rediscovered why it existed, the Bureau would erase the capability to care about the answer. Not by punishment. By irrelevance.

In District Seven, Ardent Voss felt the change before anyone else did. The disc within his chest pulsed once. The Reckoning hall trembled. People staggered as if the floor had shifted beneath them. Some raised hands to their temples. Others looked up with confusion.

Ardent did not panic. The disc had altered him. Purpose was no longer an idea. It was a direction inside his bones.

"They have begun," he said.

The Ones Who Remember watched him. None spoke. Words were fragile things in a moment like this.

Ardent moved to the obsidian slab. The symbols etched by purpose glowed faintly. He placed his hand upon its surface. The disc inside him resonated and answered. The slab steadied. The hall calmed.

Outside, the city changed.

Correction Protocol was not a weapon. Weapons destroy bodies and create martyrs. The Bureau avoided martyrs. Martyrs generate meaning. Correction Protocol dissolved relevance at the root. It broke the connection between intention and action. It did not tell citizens what to think. It removed their reason to think it.

A soft invisible lattice appeared over the Halo. It hummed across rooftops and flowed into streets. People continued to move, speak, and breathe, but the air lost something. Not oxygen. Orientation.

A man stared at his reflection in a shop window. He recognized his face and forgot why it mattered. A woman at a bus station looked at her destination and felt no reason to go. A child dropped a toy and did not bend to pick it up. Nothing was wrong. Nothing was right. The Protocol removed the axis that divided the two.

Seren Hale watched the readouts stabilize. Cognitive resonance weakened across the Halo. Personality engagement dropped. Motivational anchors dissolved. The Protocol was working.

She turned away from the primary display and accessed a sealed archive. She did not know why she opened it. That was strange. Seren always knew why. The Bureau trained her to know.

The archive asked for identification. She pressed her palm to the panel. The system hesitated. That hesitation carried weight. Systems did not hesitate. Systems executed.

The panel accepted her access.

A list appeared.

The Twelve Founder Worlds

Seren frowned. She had heard the phrase only once during her indoctrination. It was spoken as reference, not explanation. She believed the Founders were theoretical. Now their names sparked across the screen.

Varex. Solenne. Kytheron. Ilithar. Drethis. Mornexa. Aethri Prime. Yurath. Neraxis. Phron. Tembran. Khaleron.

Each name was marked with a symbol. Not decoration. Authority.

She opened the entry for Khaleron. The file revealed the origin of the Exchange.

The Twelve were ancient by human standards. Their worlds survived the Great Catastrophe, when civilizational economies collapsed not from hunger, nor plague, nor war, but from meaning itself. Species had begun trading concepts. Ownership. Memory. Belief. Purpose. When meaning became currency, reality fractured. Entire civilizations evaporated when their people forgot why they lived. Chaos threatened everything.

The Twelve formed the Exchange. They created rules for metaphysical value. They declared that nothing in existence could hold meaning without cost. Thought became debt. Purpose became liability. Identity became regulated property.

Seren scrolled. A line of text appeared that chilled her.

A species that generates purpose without authorization threatens the Exchange.

She understood. The Bureau did not prevent destruction. It prevented deviation. The Audit was not a test of survival. It was a test of compliance. The universe feared meaning. Meaning led to change. Change threatened equilibrium.

Seren closed the archive.

Ardent Voss was not a fugitive. He was a deviation.

He was debt.

In District Seven, Ardent raised his voice.

"Hold your reasons. Speak them. Anchor them."

The Reckoning obeyed, not because they were commanded, but because they understood.

Voices filled the hall.

"I am here to protect what I love."

"I am here because existence deserves more than obedience."

"I am here so the world can choose."

The slab shone brighter. The symbols aligned. The disc pulsed like a second sunrise. The Correction Protocol faltered. Citizens across District Seven blinked and asked questions they had not asked in generations. Children looked at their parents and asked why. Adults paused in work and wondered why work existed at all.

Purpose did not destroy Correction Protocol. Purpose rewrote it.

In the Spire, the technician gasped.

"Director. Sector Seven is generating counter resonance. It is constructing identity instead of dissolving it."

Seren gripped the console. "Impossible."

The technician's voice trembled. "It appears they are using meaning as structure."

Seren stared at the screen.

Meaning was not supposed to be structural. Meaning was dynamic, irrational, dangerous. It was the only currency the Exchange could not predict.

Ardent understood something the Founders feared.

Purpose was not passive.

Purpose was a force.

The Reckoning marched from the hall. Hundreds followed. Not soldiers. Not rebels. People who remembered they were alive.

Ardent spoke.

"Humanity does not survive by surrendering why. Humanity survives by creating it."

The words carried. No amplification. No broadcast. Purpose was its own signal.

Across District Seven, faces lifted. Eyes changed. Orientation returned.

The Bureau had not created obedience.

It had created hunger.

And hunger was awakening.

Seren stood perfectly still as the technician whispered.

"If they succeed, the Audit will change."

Seren's voice was raw.

"No. If they succeed, humanity will change. The Exchange will not accept that."

She looked at the Correction Protocol status. It flickered like a failing star.

For the first time in her life, Seren Hale felt something unfamiliar.

Not fear.

Recognition.

She had seen humanity without purpose.

Now she was seeing humanity with it.

And there was no turning back.

The Reckoning did not raise weapons.

The Reckoning raised a question.

Why.

The Bureau could silence thoughts. The Bureau could dissolve identity. The Bureau could flatten meaning.

But it could not answer the question it had forbidden.

It could not stop what had already begun.

The Correction Protocol was failing.

Humanity was waking.

The Exchange was watching.

And Ardent Voss was no longer alone.

The Reckoning of Why had entered the world.

It would not leave quietly.

CHAPTER THIRTEEN

THE EXCHANGE SPEAKS

The night did not fall. It recalibrated.

Colors withdrew into themselves. Buildings, once concrete in purpose, lost conviction in their outlines. Streetlights surrendered their glow, not by flickering out, but by forgetting the reason they had ever illuminated anything. Conversations faltered mid syllable. People lifted their heads with the expression of someone who suddenly realizes they are dreaming in the wrong world.

Purpose had paused.

Ardent Voss felt the shift before it crossed the senses of anyone else. The disc within his chest pulsed in rhythm with something vast and watching. The pulse was not steady. It felt like a heartbeat that was deciding if it belonged to him or something else. He inhaled sharply. He was no longer certain that his breath was a choice.

Fear arrived quietly. It was not fear of death or failure. It was the fear of dissolving into the thing he carried. A man can share his thoughts with an idea. He cannot survive becoming one. Ardent wondered if he was losing the boundary between his self and the disc's memory. He wondered if the memory was replacing him.

He wondered if Seren ever felt this before she aligned her entire existence with the Bureau.

He had loved her once, not in rebellion, but in recognition. Seren had seen the part of him that refused to remain silent. Now he could no longer tell if she was his memory or his regret.

The sky changed.

It did not tear or roar. It folded inward, as if fabric realized it was being observed and recoiled from exposure. Layer upon layer of reality bent toward an unseen center. The stars blurred into streaks. Every surface in the Halo reflected a pale, trembling light, as though the city had forgotten how to reflect anything else.

Then the world listened.

It did not freeze. It anticipated.

A presence filled the air. It was not a thing. It was a realization.

Humanity was being noticed.

Screens across the Halo flickered, paused, then emptied of content. Words dissolved mid transmission. Voices died inside throats that did not know why they had gone silent. Even thoughts hesitated, as if waiting for instruction.

Then came the voice.

It was not loud. It was not soft. It had no emotional contour. It existed as judgment.

"Humanity has violated equilibrium."

The sound was not heard through ears. It arrived in the architecture of cognition itself. No one misunderstood it.

Equilibrium had been disturbed.

Seren Hale heard those words inside the Spire and felt her posture falter. She had been trained to anticipate anomaly. She had not been trained to feel implicated by it. Her heart tightened in her chest. Not with fear. With recognition.

The Exchange only spoke when a species became dangerous.

Ardent answered before he even realized his mouth had moved.

"Humanity rediscovered intention."

The silence that followed carried weight. It pressed against the world like a hand asking whether resistance was worth the bruise.

The Exchange replied.

"Intention is not debt. Intention is risk. Debt demands accounting. Risk demands consequence."

Ardent's knees weakened. Something pressed inside his skull. It was not pain. It was containment. It was a request to return to ignorance. A suggestion that peace was easier than purpose.

For a moment, he considered surrender. He imagined walking back into the comfort of the Bureau's logic. He imagined returning to Seren, not as an equal, but as someone relieved of responsibility. He imagined letting someone else carry the question of why.

His heart twisted. Serenity had once held his face with hands that trembled not from affection, but from fear. She had told him the world does not survive meaning. It survives containment.

He had not understood her then.

He did now.

He refused the pressure.

"Meaning is not a balance sheet. It cannot be reconciled."

The Exchange did not argue.

It answered with manifestation.

Light condensed into lines. Lines folded into geometry. Geometry accepted existence. A figure emerged, not constructed of body or matter, but of decision.

A Custodian.

Its presence was precise. Its shape contained certainty. It stood as if the universe had drawn a conclusion and given it form.

Seren gasped. Training whispered that Custodians only appeared when a species threatened the ledger. Humanity had been categorized as a debtor species for centuries. A debtor species was predictable. A danger only to itself.

Now it was something else.

The Custodian spoke, and the world listened.

"You do not create meaning. You assign it. Meaning is older than your species."

Ardent felt heat rise beneath his skin. Anger. He had forgotten what anger felt like. The Bureau had trimmed such feelings from him long ago. Yet here it was. Raw. Alive. His pulse answered with force.

"You fear us because we create belief. Belief turns meaning into direction. Direction cannot be priced."

The Custodian hesitated.

The hesitation was microscopic, but it existed. Ardent saw it. Seren saw it. The world saw it.

Perfection had cracked.

The Custodian lifted its hand. Symbols appeared in the air. Law revealed itself.

THE AUDIT ASSESSMENT

One: A species must acknowledge debt

Two: A species must correct imbalance

Three: A species must relinquish claims it cannot sustain

Four: A species must not create new variables

Ardent read the rules, and the world felt smaller. He looked at the Reckoning. Their expressions changed from curiosity into realization.

"We are the variable."

The Custodian responded.

"You created purpose without authorization. Purpose without precedent. Purpose without debt."

Ardent stepped forward.

"It is ours because no one gave it to us."

The Custodian flickered again.

"Ownership implies cost."

Ardent laughed once. It was not humor. It was despair turned insight.

"Not if the value did not exist before we made it."

Seren felt something break inside her. The Bureau had never been wrong. It had been terrified of the answer to a single question.

What happens when a species invents meaning?

The Exchange spoke.

"Humanity challenges the ledger."

Ardent replied.

"The ledger is afraid of becoming a story."

Silence spread like dawn.

The Custodian released a new command.

CORRECTION DENIED. ESCALATION INITIATED.

Fear rippled through the Reckoning. Ardent saw it. He felt it. He did not fight it. Emotion was not the enemy. It was evidence that they were not yet undone.

The Custodian's voice changed. It carried something unexpected.

Curiosity.

"You are no longer a debtor species. You are an origin species."

Ardent's chest tightened. The disc pulsed in agreement. He was not ready for this destiny. He did not want it. He wanted Seren standing beside him, telling him this was not madness. He wanted his old life, where numbers behaved and purpose did not breathe.

He wanted simplicity.

Simplicity was gone.

"Define origin species," he said.

"A species that generates meaning instead of inheriting it."

Ardent closed his eyes. The world narrowed. His life became a single thread connecting the Bureau, the disc, the memory of Seren's lips, and the truth he could no longer surrender.

"And the Audit?"

"An origin species is not audited. It is challenged."

"Challenged by what?"

The answer came from beyond stars.

"Everything that believes meaning belongs to it."

Seren's pulse fractured. She understood the Bureau at last. It did not protect humanity from destruction. It protected the universe from what humanity might become.

The Custodian dissolved. Only a line remained.

THE AUDIT IS CANCELLED. THE CONTEST BEGINS.

Ardent inhaled. His voice did not shout. It carried the weight of a decision that would outlive him.

"This is not a test of debt. This is a challenge to prove why we exist."

The Reckoning did not cheer.

Belief does not need sound.

Belief needs direction.

The night darkened, yet humanity did not shrink.

For the first time in history, humanity faced the universe without apology.

It did not tremble.

It answered.

CHAPTER FOURTEEN

THE FIRST CLAIMANT

Humanity did not celebrate its elevation.

Celebration belongs to events that people understand. The Exchange had spoken. The Custodian had appeared. The Audit had been cancelled. The Contest had begun. None of those words had settled into the human mind yet. They hovered above understanding like storm clouds that had not decided where to break.

District Seven sat in an uneasy stillness. Streets that once pulsed with routine now felt like corridors inside a waiting organism. Windows glowed in scattered patterns, as though the city itself could not decide whether it should be awake or asleep. The air held a quality that did not exist before. It felt like expectation.

Ardent Voss stood in the center of the plaza with the Reckoning gathered around him. They were no longer simply the Ones Who Remember. Word had spread through the district. People who had never met him had come. Some wore uniforms. Some wore work clothes. Some arrived barefoot, having stepped out of their homes in the middle of whatever they were doing when the sky changed. They all carried one thing in common.

They were afraid of going back to what they had been.

Ardent's hands were steady, but his chest was not. The disc within him pulsed in a rhythm that did not match his heartbeat. Sometimes it ran faster, as if reaching for something he did not yet see. Sometimes it slowed, as if waiting for him to catch up. He no longer knew whether he was driving his purpose or being driven by it.

He remembered the first time he held Seren's hand. It had not been in the darkness of her private chamber. It had been in a corridor, years before that night. She had slipped a data slate from his fingers in a transfer gesture so common that no one else noticed. Her fingers had lingered for a fraction of a second longer than necessary. In that moment he had felt seen. Not as an auditor. Not as a tool. As a person.

He wondered if she had felt the same way or if that had always been his illusion.

Now she was somewhere above him in the Spire, surrounded by surveillance feeds and protocols. He was here in the open, surrounded by people who thought he knew what he was doing. The distance between them had become more than measurable space. It had become ideology.

Someone tugged at his sleeve.

Ardent turned. An elderly woman with deep lines around her eyes looked up at him. Her voice was quiet, but it carried.

"Is this real," she asked, "or will they fix us back to how we were?"

He forced himself to meet her gaze. "They will try."

"Can they succeed?"

Ardent hesitated.

The disc inside him thrummed. It would have answered for him if he let it. He refused that, for now. He did not want to become a mouthpiece for a memory, no matter how ancient. He wanted his answer to be his own.

"They can only succeed," he said, "if we decide we are tired of choosing."

The woman nodded slowly. "Choosing is exhausting."

"It is," Ardent agreed. "So is breathing. We have never decided to stop."

The ghost of a smile touched her lips. She stepped back into the crowd.

A murmur moved through District Seven. It was not language. It was sensation. The air grew thicker. Shadows sharpened. A strange hush descended, not the silence of absence, but the silence of the moment before a verdict.

Someone behind him whispered, "It feels like we are being read."

Ardent felt it too. The sensation of being inside a thought that was not his own. The Exchange had declared the Contest. That declaration had been abstract. Now the abstraction was focusing.

Far above, in the Spire's command chamber, Seren Hale watched District Seven on a primary screen. She had expanded the plaza feed until Ardent's figure occupied the center. She could see the lines of strain around his mouth. To anyone else he might have looked resolute. To her, he looked haunted.

She placed a hand on the console, not for balance, but to ground herself in something physical.

"Zoom out," she ordered softly.

The technician complied. The view expanded to show the curve of the district, then the broader ring of the Halo. Lights pulsed across the orbital arcs. Lines of energy from the Projection Grid still lingered, fragments of the Correction Protocol that had failed to erase intention.

Seren's fingers curled. She could feel a thought at the edge of her mind, one she did not allow herself to complete.

What if Ardent is right?

She killed the thought. Doubt was not permitted at her level. Doubt was a virus. Doubt spread. Doubt made systems collapse.

But the Exchange had spoken. The Custodian had appeared. The Audit was cancelled. The rules had changed. Her training had never covered this.

The air in the Spire shifted. Screens flickered with static for a single heartbeat. Lights dimmed without losing power. The atmosphere pressed inward, as if something very large and very far away had turned its attention toward this single point in space.

In the plaza, people raised their heads again.

The sky no longer held stars as individual points. They smeared, as if some invisible hand had dragged them across velvet. Clouds pulled inward. The night bent toward a seam that had not existed before and should never have existed at all.

Ardent's breath caught. The disc surged. He knew, even before it happened, what this meant.

Opposition had arrived.

The sky fractured along a single line of light. It was not hot. It was not bright. It was sharp. The fracture widened, not like a wound, but like an invitation reluctantly granted.

Beyond that crack lay a darkness that did not resemble absence. It resembled attention.

From that darkness, something stepped.

The Reckoning did not scream. They could not. The part of the mind that chose how to react had not yet found a valid response. The figure that emerged from the fracture did not conform to any known category. It resembled a person only because the human brain insisted on coherence.

Its body seemed carved from starlight and negation, alternating strands of illumination and void. Its edges wavered between presence and absence. Wherever its eyes should have been, there were instead fixed points in reality where awareness concentrated.

Ardent felt his heart constrict. This was not the Custodian. This was not the Exchange speaking through law. This was something else. An agent. A participant. A claimant.

Seren watched from the Spire, breath shallow. The feed struggled to interpret the figure. Its lines blurred on the screen. Algorithms tried to stabilize it and failed. The system rendered approximation. Her mind rejected it.

"Director," the technician whispered, "the visual cannot resolve the entity. We are seeing a compression of variables."

Seren said nothing. Her eyes never left Ardent.

The being in the sky spoke.

"Humanity claims purpose."

The words did not accuse. They recognized.

Ardent stepped forward, every muscle tense.

"Yes," he said. His voice did not shake. His fear did, but his voice did not. "We do."

The figure tilted its head. The motion felt like a question deciding how sharp it should become.

"Your species invents meaning," it said. "You believe meaning is choice. You have created a why without precedent."

Ardent held steady.

"Meaning is not found," he replied. "Meaning is made."

The figure answered without delay.

"Incorrect. Meaning is owned. Meaning is inherited. Meaning is assigned. Species do not create purpose. They serve it."

The Reckoning shifted uneasily. Many had grown under Bureau doctrine. Some still carried fragments of its language. The claim that purpose was property did not feel new. It felt like an old rule returning with teeth.

Ardent raised a hand. The crowd quieted.

"Who are you?" he asked.

The figure replied.

"I am Kolinar of the Archivist Domain."

The name vibrated in the air. The Archivist Domain. Ardent had seen the phrase only in restricted files. A civilization recorded in the Exchange's most ancient agreements. A species that had survived its Audit.

Kolinar continued.

"My species was the first to be judged worthy of purpose."

Ardent frowned. "You mean the first to be allowed to wield meaning."

Kolinar nodded slightly.

"Purpose is not universal. It is a regulated resource. It was granted to us after our equilibrium was proven. We hold custodial claim. You are trespassing."

Ardent took a careful breath. Every instinct told him that this conversation was more dangerous than any weapon the Bureau had ever built.

"We are not taking what is yours," he said slowly. "We are making what is ours."

Kolinar's form sharpened.

"Purpose that is self made is counterfeit. It lacks origin. It lacks authority. It lacks permanence."

Ardent felt something surge within him. Grief for a future that could vanish, anger for a past that had been stolen, fear of becoming a symbol instead of a man.

"Authority is a story we tell to avoid responsibility," he replied. "Permanence is a comfort we invented to avoid change. We chose meaning. That choice is our authority."

Kolinar's shape flickered, as if a pattern in its structure had misaligned.

"You confuse desire with right," it said. "Only species recognized by the Exchange may wield meaning. Humanity was not selected."

Ardent nodded once.

"Exactly," he said quietly. "That is why we had to choose it. Permission is not purpose. Permission is control."

A murmur swept through the plaza. Seren heard it even through the feed. It shook her more than Kolinar's presence did. Humanity was listening to Ardent. Not out of fear. Out of recognition.

Kolinar stepped closer. The air tightened. The sky pressed downward.

"You threaten the ledger," it said. "You threaten the balance. You threaten history."

Ardent answered with an unexpected calm.

"History is not balance. History is direction. We are choosing ours."

Kolinar's form surged with light and shadow.

"You speak as though purpose can be created by voice."

Ardent placed his hand over his heart.

"Purpose is created by choice," he said. "My voice is only the sound of that choice."

The disc inside him pulsed hard. A wave of light rippled through his body and out into the air. Far away, in the hall beneath the district, the obsidian slab trembled.

Kolinar recoiled.

"Your meaning resonates," it said. "It is unstructured. It is unstable. It should collapse."

Ardent could not help it. He smiled.

"Meaning is not stable," he answered. "That is why it changes things."

The crowd breathed as one. The air shifted.

The Contest had begun.

The First Contest

Kolinar raised both hands. The night sky rippled like a disturbed reflection. A wave of pressure formed around its body and rolled outward, aimed not at flesh, but at certainty. It moved through the plaza like a cold wind that no one could feel on their skin and everyone could feel inside their thoughts.

The Reckoning staggered. Memories blurred. Intentions frayed around the edges. Questions lost their center. Confidence evaporated without being replaced by anything.

One man sank to his knees, clutching his head. "Why did I come here?" he gasped. "What was I expecting?"

A woman beside him stared at Ardent. "Who is he? Why are we listening to him?"

The wave did not erase memories. It stripped them of relevance. It attacked the link between choice and meaning. It made everything feel optional, unimportant, unanchored.

From the Spire, Seren watched the readouts in horror.

"Director," a technician stammered. "Sector Seven cognitive coherence is collapsing."

Seren saw it in the data.

Patterns frayed. Focus dissolved. Neural engagement destabilized.

Her training told her this was exactly what should happen. An unrecognized species claiming purpose should collapse under the weight of its own presumption. Meaning without permission should implode.

But Ardent was still standing.

He felt the wave pass through his mind. For a moment, thoughts slipped away from him like water poured over polished stone. The fears he carried no longer gripped him. The hopes he cherished no longer drove him. Everything flattened into a gentle grey plane of possibility that required nothing of him.

It was almost peaceful.

He could stop.

He could let go of the disc, let go of the Reckoning, let go of meaning. He could return to the life he once had, where rules were clear and emotions were trimmed to fit policy.

Seren's face appeared behind his eyes. Not the version of her crafted by Bureau projection, but the one from Edelon, after their bodies had betrayed their oaths. She had asked him, voice cracking, whether purpose was worth annihilation. He had never answered.

Now he did.

Yes.

The disc inside him burned. Heat spread through his ribs. His vision blurred, then sharpened. The wave of pressure shattered against something that was not idea, not doctrine, not memory.

It was decision.

Ardent shouted, his voice cutting through the plaza.

"Hold your reasons. Speak them. Anchor them."

The Reckoning flinched, as if waking from a near drowning.

A woman near the front shouted, voice shaking.

"I am here to protect the people I love."

A young man followed.

"I am here because I refuse to live as someone else's equation."

An older worker raised his head.

"I am here so my grandchildren will not inherit emptiness."

A child whispered, almost too softly to hear.

"I am here because I want my life to matter."

Each declaration struck the wave like a stone thrown into moving water. The pressure faltered. The air shimmered with lines of light, each line connecting a voice to a reason.

The obsidian slab in the hall flared to life. Symbols rearranged. Phrases appeared.

Choice creates origin.

Origin creates direction.

Direction creates meaning.

Kolinar's form wavered.

"You cannot anchor meaning without inheritance," it said. "You have no origin."

Ardent took a step forward, his fear burning into clarity.

"Our origin," he shouted, "is the moment we decided we deserved one."

The wave collapsed.

The plaza steadied. The people did not simply recover. They solidified.

Seren's breath escaped her in a sound that was almost a sob. She covered her mouth quickly, but the technician looked up at her anyway.

"Director?" he asked quietly.

She straightened. Her voice regained its practiced calm.

"Continue observation," she said. "No interference."

The technician frowned. "Should we not assist the claimant?"

Seren's jaw tightened.

"We interfere when debt is in question," she answered. "This is not about debt anymore. This is about definition."

On the screen, Ardent was still speaking.

"Purpose is not granted," he said. "Purpose is claimed. Humanity exists because we decide existence has value."

Kolinar's form trembled. Doubt entered its outline like cracks in glass.

"You believe choice outranks origin," it said.

Ardent did not hesitate.

"Choice creates origin."

The crowd gasped. Not because they understood all the implications, but because they felt the statement resonate in the part of them that had always resisted being told who they were.

The city lights flickered in response. Not in fear. In alignment.

Kolinar stepped back.

"This violates the Exchange," it said. There was less certainty in its tone now. More something else.

Something closer to unease.

Ardent lifted his chin.

"Then the Exchange must evolve."

Silence fell again.

For a long moment, nothing moved. The fracture in the sky held open like a wound waiting to decide whether it would heal or spread.

Kolinar regarded Ardent. When it spoke again, its tone had changed. The disdain remained, but beneath it, there was something almost like reluctant respect.

"You have made a claim," it said. "The first of the Contest. Humanity declares that meaning can be generated without inheritance."

Ardent nodded once.

"Yes."

Kolinar's form began to dissipate into strands of light that drifted upward toward the fracture.

"Then your claim must be contested," it said. "Others will come. Not because they hate you. Because they cannot allow your definition of meaning to stand untested."

Ardent swallowed.

"We will meet them."

Kolinar vanished. The fracture in the sky closed. The stars reappeared, though they did not look the same. The night felt thinner, as if something had passed through it and taken a layer of illusion away.

A single line of faint text remained above the Halo.

Humanity has made a claim. It will be answered.

The Reckoning Understands

Sound returned slowly. People shifted. The city exhaled.

The Reckoning gathered closer to Ardent. Their faces showed exhaustion, fear, and something fragile that refused to die.

Hope.

A young girl with ink stained fingers pointed at the sky.

"What happens now?" she asked.

Ardent looked up. He wished, for one moment, that he could say something comforting. Something simple. Something small.

He had no such luxury.

"Now," he said quietly, "others will come."

"Who are they?" a man asked. His voice was steadier than his hands.

"Any species," Ardent answered, "that believes meaning belongs to it. Anyone who has built their existence on the assumption that purpose is property."

The woman with bright, clear eyes, the one who had first greeted him at the Refuge of Unfinished Thoughts, stepped to his side.

"And what do we do when they come?"

Ardent thought of Seren, watching from above. He thought of the Bureau, trying to maintain a protective prison around a species that wanted to leave it. He thought of the Exchange, afraid that its ledger might turn into a story it could not control.

He thought of the disc inside his chest, pulsing not with foreign command, but with human decisions given weight by time.

"We keep creating purpose," he said. "We do not wait for permission. We do not ask for validation. We make our meaning so strong that even opposition becomes part of its proof."

He looked at each face around him.

"We do what humanity has always done when no one allows it a path. We imagine one."

The young girl frowned thoughtfully.

"Will imagining be enough?"

Ardent smiled, tired and sincere.

"It has brought every civilization in the Compact to where it stands. The difference is that we now know we are doing it."

The plaza began to move. Groups formed. Conversations ignited. Some people cried. Some laughed with a hysterical edge. Some fell silent and simply stared at their hands, as if realizing they had just held something intangible and enormous.

In the hall beneath the district, the obsidian slab cooled. The last of the symbols rearranged themselves into a single phrase:

Why we exist is created together.

Above the Contest

In the Spire, Seren Hale remained motionless as the screens normalized. The night returned to its usual configuration. District Seven settled into uneasy order. Status indicators in the command chamber drifted back within acceptable ranges.

The technician broke the silence.

"Director. Your orders?"

Seren stared at Ardent's frozen image on a paused frame. His face held no triumph. Only weight.

"For now," she said, "we do nothing. We log everything. We wait."

The technician frowned. "The Bureau was established to prevent exactly this. An unapproved actor engaging the Exchange directly. A species claiming definition without Compact authority."

Seren's lips thinned.

"The Bureau was established," she said slowly, "to ensure humanity survived its own ignorance. That has changed. We are no longer ignorant. We are dangerous."

She thought of the First Moderators. Veda Arkan, Torren Halix, Seraph Jin, Miren Voss. They had believed existence required control. They had built ITEB as a shield made of rules. They had never asked if their shield would eventually become a cage.

She remembered Miren's engraved words.

Existence is not free. Purpose is collateral.

She closed her eyes.

"Director?" the technician prompted.

Seren opened them.

"Increase passive monitoring of all districts," she said. "Do not interfere with District Seven unless directly authorized. From now on, every disruption to equilibrium may be an answer to humanity's claim. We cannot afford to confuse the Contest with a crime."

The technician nodded, unsettled.

"And Ardent Voss?" he asked.

Seren allowed herself one breath of honesty, quiet enough that only she could hear it.

"What are you doing, Ardent?" she whispered.

Then, louder.

"Flag his presence in all sectors. He is no longer merely an auditor. He is a variable. And now the universe knows his name."

She turned away from the screens, but his image followed her in memory.

In District Seven, Ardent felt the weight of eyes he could not see. Not just the Bureau's surveillance. Not just Kolinar's departing attention. Something much larger.

The Contest had its first claimant.

He did not know if humanity would win.

He only knew this.

They had finally decided to play.

And the universe, at last, would have to answer why they existed.

CHAPTER FIFTEEN

THE FRACTURE WITHIN

The slab still glowed from the last gathering. Lines of light pulsed gently beneath its dark surface, like a heartbeat pressed under stone. Every symbol etched there had once been spoken aloud by a human voice. Every curve held conviction. Every angle carried a quiet, stubborn refusal to drift through life without a reason.

Ardent Voss stood before it with his hands at his sides. He did not touch the stone. He had done that once, and the slab had answered. It had changed him. Now he watched from a measured distance, as if proximity itself demanded a level of honesty he was not sure he could afford at this moment.

The air in the hall smelled of dust, metal, and human breath layered over days of arguments, confessions, and whispered fears. Too many minds had collided here. The Reckoning had not meant to become a center, but movements always found one. Meaning draws gravity. Gravity draws consequence.

District Seven was changing.

Outside, the streets no longer moved with simple routine. People had begun to hesitate near the doorway of the hall, pausing mid stride as if they felt a soft tug from something inside. Some walked past and found themselves glancing back, confused by a sense of having almost remembered something. Others lingered near the entrance, hands in pockets, eyes on the ground, hovering as if they were waiting for permission from a voice they could not yet hear. A few crossed the threshold, sat along the walls, and listened with the tense stillness of people who suspect their lives are about to tilt.

Inside, the Ones Who Remember had grown into something larger. There were familiar faces, worn by long years under Bureau symmetry. There were new faces, sharp with recent awakening. Some eyes were filled with hope. Some were heavy with fatigue. Some watched Ardent with an expression he had never wanted: expectation.

He did not want to become anyone's answer.

He took a slow breath and turned from the slab to face them.

"We are being watched," he said.

His voice was not loud, but the room had learned to listen. Conversations quieted. The air seemed to lean forward.

"By the Bureau. By Kolinar. By the Exchange itself. They are measuring us, not by what we say, but by what we continue to choose."

A low murmur ran through the hall. Ardent saw shoulders tighten. Hands clasp. Eyes narrow.

"The Exchange does not care about our slogans," he continued. "It cares whether our meaning can survive pressure. The Bureau has always been that pressure. Kolinar is now the test. The Exchange is the one who watches and writes the result."

He let that sink in.

"But the most dangerous pressure does not come from outside. It comes from here." He tapped his chest lightly. "From inside."

A young woman near the front frowned. "Why inside?"

"Because purpose divides before it unites," Ardent said. "Before we can carry a reason for humanity, we must accept that not everyone will want it. Some will choose safety over meaning. Some will choose quiet over questions. Some will choose borrowed purpose because it feels easier than making their own."

Silence settled for a moment, not empty but thoughtful.

Someone in the back muttered, "So the danger is us."

It was a statement, not quite a challenge. The room shifted toward the voice, parting to reveal the speaker.

Deren Sol stepped into the open.

Former Bureau analyst. Tall, broad shouldered, with the posture of a man trained to stand only where models and projections supported his presence. His eyes were sharp, his jaw firm, his expression composed. Ardent had noticed him in earlier gatherings, always near the back, absorbing everything, offering nothing.

Today he had chosen to speak.

Ardent nodded. "The danger is what we do with meaning. Yes."

Deren halted a few steps from the slab and looked around. He spoke with the clarity of someone used to explaining complicated truths to people who did not want to hear them.

"You woke people up," Deren said. "You told them purpose belongs to them. You told them they can choose their own reasons. That feels beautiful. It feels powerful." He gestured toward the slab. "It also feels like the opening chapter of every catastrophe we have ever crafted."

A few people tensed. Others listened more intently.

Ardent answered, "Catastrophe came when purpose was decided for us."

Deren shook his head lightly. "That is part of the story. Not the whole. I spent years inside the Bureau reading long term projections and cultural simulations. Every time humanity believed it had found a great reason to exist, it fractured. Those who were certain they knew why turned against those who did not agree. Righteousness against heresy. Enlightened against ignorant. Saved against condemned."

He looked back at Ardent.

"Do you really think this time will be different?"

"We are not building one dogma," Ardent said. "We are encouraging people to claim their own direction."

"Yes," Deren replied. "That is the part that frightens me."

He pointed at the slab.

"This looks ordered now. Those symbols seem harmonious. But every one of them is a different why. A different direction. A different claim about what matters. When pressure increases, those differences will pull against each other. Belief becomes boundary. Boundary becomes conflict."

A few heads nodded. Others shook.

Ardent held his gaze. "So your answer is to give our meaning to someone else and ask them to manage it for us."

"If they are better suited to it than we are," Deren said, "yes."

Murmurs rose. Some curious. Some angry. Some relieved that someone had finally spoken what they feared.

Ardent asked, "Better suited in what way?"

"Experience," Deren said. "Authority. Recognition. Kolinar was the first species judged worthy of purpose. They have already survived an Audit. They have already proven their meaning. The Exchange trusts them."

Something in the room tightened.

"You have spoken with them," Ardent said quietly.

Deren did not look away. "I have. While you were reaching upward, I reached sideways. I wanted to know if there was a path that did not end with us shattered by our own contradictions."

He spread his hands, palms open.

"Kolinar offers structure. They say humanity does not need to create meaning from nothing. We can inherit a portion of theirs. We can live under their purpose. Protected. Guided."

Ardent heard the pull of the idea. He could feel others hearing it too. Safety wrapped in legitimacy. Survival wrapped in validation.

"Under their purpose," Ardent repeated. "Which makes us what?"

Deren answered in a single word.

"Safe."

Ardent shook his head. "It makes us dependent. It makes us an extension of another species. If our reason to exist comes from them, we are not human. We are a cultural annex."

Deren's lips curved into a thin, almost kind smile.

"And what are we under the Exchange now? Equal participants?"

Ardent did not respond immediately. Deren pressed on.

"Be honest. We have never been free. The Council traded our origin. The Bureau shaped us. The Exchange waited to erase or correct us. You did not break a system. You stepped out of one cage into an open field and invited everyone to run, without telling them the storm above is still there."

He stepped closer, close enough that Ardent could see the fine stress lines near his eyes.

"You are playing with the same force that turned Edelon into a hollow species. You want us to believe we can handle what they could not. I respect the courage. I do not share the optimism."

Behind Deren, some people shifted, as if moving physically closer to his certainty.

Ardent felt the weight of their uncertainty press against his ribs.

"You think Kolinar will save us," he said. "Why would they?"

"Because they fear what will happen if we fail," Deren said. "Kolinar does not want humanity erased. They want us contained. They believe meaning is territory. If we try to claim our own and collapse, the chaos will spread. They would rather adopt us than risk an uncontrolled failure."

He turned slightly, addressing the room.

"I am not against meaning," Deren said. "I am against pretending we can conjure it from nothing and not pay a price that kills us. Kolinar understands the cost. They have already paid it. I would rather stand under the shelter of a proven purpose than gamble that we can invent one strong enough in a single age to satisfy the Exchange."

The words landed heavily. You could almost hear them settle into minds.

Several people nodded. Some crossed their arms. A few, for the first time, looked at Ardent not as a savior, but as a risk.

Ardent's chest ached. He remembered Edelon. The hollow city. The people whose identities had been edited until they no longer remembered how to ask why. He remembered Seren's face there, tight with sorrow and conviction. He remembered the night in her chamber, the question she had asked him that he had never dared answer.

Is purpose worth annihilation?

He had avoided the answer then.

He could not avoid it now.

"Deren," Ardent said softly, "you are afraid of us."

Deren held his gaze. "I am afraid of unsupervised freedom. I am afraid of a species that has never handled power well now being told that its inner desire is sacred."

He motioned toward the slab.

"This makes people feel noble. It gives them language for the ache they have always carried. But when the Exchange returns and demands a reason, what will we do? Present a thousand different whys and hope they do not pull us apart?"

"We are not trying to collapse into one sentence," Ardent said. "We are trying to agree on one direction. A shared understanding that existence deserves meaning."

Deren shook his head slowly. "The Exchange does not assess direction. It assesses statement. Kolinar believes they can help give us one. You believe we can build it from scratch. I do not trust humanity as architect."

Silence stretched, heavy and alive.

Ardent finally asked, "So what are you saying? That you want to leave?"

Deren nodded.

"Yes. And I am not going alone."

He lifted his hand.

For a heartbeat nothing happened.

Then one woman stepped away from the group and stood behind him.

Then a man.

Then three more.

Then ten.

Familiar faces. Sera, who had once cried while explaining her fear of dying without ever making anything that mattered. Joran, who had argued passionately that love was the purest form of why. An older woman who had never spoken in public, but whose eyes always burned in the second row.

They all moved to stand with Deren.

Ardent felt the loss like a physical cut he had not braced for.

He swallowed.

"This is your choice," he said. "I will not stop you. I cannot claim to believe in purpose and then deny yours."

Respect flickered briefly in Deren's eyes.

"That is the first honest thing you have said since you lit this fire," Deren said quietly.

He turned back to the others.

"You are brave," he told those who stayed. "Maybe you are right. Maybe humanity can carry its own meaning. I hope so, I truly do. But I will not risk the entire species on hope."

He faced Ardent again.

"Kolinar has offered a path. They will recognize those who align with their purpose. We will gain standing in the Exchange under their protection. If we succeed, we will live. If you fail, at least some of us will continue."

Ardent asked, "And if Kolinar is not a guardian, but a collector?"

Deren's jaw tightened.

"Then at least we will have made a choice we understood."

He walked toward the door.

The defectors followed.

No one blocked their path. No one tried to argue them back.

The door slid open with a soft whisper. Light from the street drew their shapes into silhouettes for a moment.

Then they were gone.

The door closed.

The hall felt larger. Emptier. Heavier.

No one spoke.

Ardent turned back to the slab. Some of the symbols had dimmed. Not extinguished, but faint, like distant stars hidden by cloud. Every faded mark represented a voice now walking a different road.

Meaning had fractured.

Not across species.

Across humanity.

The woman with bright eyes, the one who had greeted him on his first arrival, stepped closer.

"Are we weaker now?" she asked.

Ardent stared at the dim patches on the stone. The ache in his chest deepened, but beneath it was something else. Clarity.

"No," he said at last. "We are clearer. Purpose will always divide. It has to. A reason that cannot be refused is not a reason. It is an order."

He reached out and placed his palm on the slab.

The symbols pulsed in response. Not as bright as before. Not as many. But real.

"We have to accept this," Ardent said. "Some will align with Kolinar. Some will trust the Bureau. Some will choose quiet. Some will choose nothing. We cannot own every path."

He looked up, meeting the gaze of each person still present.

"But we are still here. We are still choosing. That means the Reckoning is not a crowd. It is a decision."

A low breath moved through the room, a blend of grief and relief.

Outside, the city hummed, unaware of the fault line that had just opened in its soul.

Inside the hall, the fracture settled.

This was not a failure.

It was a cost.

Meaning always had one.

Ardent closed his eyes for a moment, then opened them with a new, sharpened resolve.

"We go on," he said. "Not because we are sure we are right. We go on because this is the only way to be human that I can live with."

The Ones Who Remained nodded.

Not in perfect unison.

In honest agreement.

The Reckoning still existed.

Smaller.

Stronger.

Clearer.

High above District Seven, the Spire stood like a blade of light driven into the heart of Halo. It was the tallest structure in the city and the only one that never seemed to cast a true shadow. Seven levels rose within it, each narrower than the one below, each devoted to a different aspect of control.

The first level softened visitors and dissolved confidence.

The second measured behavior and rewrote patterns.

The third curated memory.

The fourth reshaped identity.

The fifth guided narrative.

The sixth commanded compliance.

The seventh, far above all, held silence that no one described.

Seren Hale stood in the Director's Atria on Level Six. The floor beneath her feet was transparent, revealing the levels below like layers of a single carefully managed mind. Agents moved along corridors. Screens flickered. Decisions flowed upward to her station.

Beside her stood Senior Compliance Adjutant Jalen Rhyse, his posture exact, his hands clasped behind his back, his silver eyes reflecting the live feed of District Seven.

"There is a measurable reduction in total headcount inside the gathering hall," Jalen observed. "The movement is naturally consolidating."

Seren watched Ardent on the central screen. Saw the way his shoulders had tensed when people left. Saw the way he steadied himself afterward. To anyone else he might have looked composed. To her, he looked like a man carrying something that hurt and choosing not to set it down.

"Consolidation is not always weakness," she said. "Sometimes it is recognition."

Jalen tilted his head slightly. "Fragmentation of belief typically reduces threat potential. Those who aligned with this Kolinar representative may become manageable. Those who remain with Voss will be fewer."

Seren said nothing.

Jalen glanced at her. "Director. Your orders?"

She did not answer immediately. Her eyes stayed on Ardent.

She thought of the night at Edelon. The way he had looked at her as though the world had peeled open. The way his hands had trembled when they first touched. She had believed then that nothing lasting could come from them. The Audit would erase whatever they felt.

Now the Audit was gone.

He had not come back to her.

"Leave me," she said quietly.

Jalen blinked once. "Director?"

"Leave me. That is an order."

Jalen bowed his head. "Yes, Director."

He walked from the room. The door closed with a soft hiss.

The command chamber hummed softly. Lights glowed, steady and perfect. The Spire was built to eliminate shadows, but somehow one had grown inside her chest.

Seren stepped forward until she stood directly over the section of transparent floor that aligned above District Seven. Far below, the hall appeared as a small rectangle of faint light.

She placed her hand on the glass.

"Ardent," she whispered. The name left her lips as if it had been waiting a very long time to escape.

She did not fear what he was becoming.

She feared what he was leaving her in.

An ordered world she had helped design.

A system that now felt less like protection and more like denial.

She had chosen the Bureau once.

She did not know if she would choose it again.

Not yet.

In the streets, Deren led his group away from the hall. No one spoke for a while. Their footsteps rang against stone and metal, a single shared rhythm of reluctant resolve.

Sera broke the silence first. "Do you think Ardent despises us now?"

Deren shook his head. "Ardent does not despise. That is the problem. He cares more about the idea of meaning than about the cost of chasing it."

Joran frowned. "Is that wrong?"

Deren sighed. "It is not wrong. It is dangerous."

He looked upward.

Somewhere beyond the skyline, the Exchange watched. Somewhere beyond that, Kolinar waited.

"Kolinar will receive us," Deren said. "They understand what we are asking. They understand that we are not rejecting meaning. We are outsourcing it."

He did not say the quieter truth that lodged under his tongue.

He feared they might be outsourcing more than that.

In homes and corridors across District Seven, small anomalies began to surface.

A factory worker paused in front of a blank wall that he had passed every day of his life without noticing. Today he stared at it for several minutes, unable to remember why his life felt so narrow.

A child woke from sleep with a question she could not articulate. Her parents patted her back and told her to rest. The question did not rest.

An older man who had watched the feed of the plaza from a cramped apartment placed his hand over his heart and whispered, "I do not know what my purpose is."

For the first time in his life, he added, "But I know I want one."

No one tracked these moments.

No one recorded the exact instant when a life that had been drifting decided to lean toward intention.

But something did.

Far beyond Halo, in the unseen calculus of the Exchange, probabilities shifted. Threads of prediction wavered. A ledger that once considered humanity a debtor species now struggled to categorize it.

One part of the species chose safety under Kolinar's shadow.

One part chose self made meaning and risk.

The numbers did not align as they should.

Something like curiosity stirred in the cold machinery of cosmic judgment.

The Contest had barely begun.

Already, humanity had done something no model had accurately projected.

It had split its bet.

Back in the hall of unfinished thoughts, Ardent stood once more before the slab. The remaining Reckoning gathered around him. They were fewer now. They were also, in a way, revealed.

The woman with bright eyes stood at his side.

"Are we enough?" she asked again, softer this time.

Ardent did not look at the exit. He did not look at the dim symbols. He looked at the people who remained.

"We do not need to be many," he said. "Purpose does not count us. It asks whether we are willing to live by what we claim."

The slab pulsed once under his hand.

"We are not a guarantee," he said. "We are not a shield. We are not a solution."

He paused.

"We are an answer."

He looked at them, and they looked back.

Not as followers.

As participants.

The fracture within humanity was real now. Clear and undeniable.

Part of the species believed that purpose should be managed by those who had already survived the test.

Part believed that purpose must be created, not borrowed.

Which side was right remained unwritten.

But one thing had become certain.

Whatever humanity became next would not happen by accident.

The Reckoning of Why would carry the question forward.

And the universe, at last, would have to respond.

CHAPTER SIXTEEN

THE WEIGHT OF CHOICE

The city did not change all at once.

That was what unsettled Ardent Voss the most.

After the fracture, after the quiet departures and the doors closing behind those who had chosen another path, District Seven did not erupt. It did not riot. It did not collapse into chaos or surge into unity. It simply adjusted, like a body absorbing a wound it had not yet decided how to heal. The absence of spectacle felt deliberate, as though the city itself were waiting to see whether the damage would demand attention or fade quietly into routine.

People still went to work. Transports still ran on schedule. Markets opened and closed. The ordinary rhythm of life continued with a precision that felt almost accusatory, as if the world itself were asking whether the choices made inside the hall truly mattered. Ardent wondered if this was how civilizations always processed existential turning points, by pretending nothing essential had shifted until the pretending itself became impossible to sustain.

He stood at the edge of the central plaza and watched faces pass.

Some people moved with the same blank efficiency they always had, eyes forward, steps measured, minds already elsewhere. Others carried a new tension, a hesitation in their gait, a lingering awareness that something unseen had shifted beneath the surface of their routines. Conversations trailed off more easily. Laughter arrived later, thinner than before. A few people stopped mid stride, glanced upward, and frowned without knowing why, as if they had briefly felt the echo of a question they could not yet name.

Meaning had not announced itself.

It had begun to press.

The Reckoning no longer felt like a place. It felt like a condition, a pressure that seeped into daily motion, altering nothing directly while quietly changing everything underneath. Ardent felt it in the way people avoided his eyes, or lingered just a fraction longer than politeness required. He felt it in the way silence now carried implication instead of absence.

Inside the hall, the slab rested dormant. Its surface no longer pulsed constantly. The symbols that remained glowed faintly, steady rather than urgent. They did not demand attention. They waited. Ardent had come to understand that waiting was not passivity. It was endurance.

He sat alone on one of the benches along the wall, elbows resting on his knees, hands loosely clasped. For the first time since he had stepped into a role he had never asked for, no one stood in front of him seeking guidance, absolution, or reassurance. The absence felt heavier than expectation ever had. He had learned how to answer questions. He had not learned how to sit with silence that expected nothing and judged everything.

He had believed the fracture would bring clarity. In some ways, it had. The illusion of unanimity was gone. The danger of believing everyone would choose risk for meaning had revealed itself without mercy. Yet clarity did not bring relief. It brought responsibility, not for the choices others made, but for the space those choices left behind.

Responsibility, he was learning, did not arrive with instructions.

A soft sound broke the quiet.

Footsteps.

Ardent looked up to see the woman with bright eyes approach. She had stayed when others left. She always did. There was resolve in her posture now, but also uncertainty she did not bother to hide. That honesty had become rare.

"They are talking about us," she said.

"Who?" Ardent asked.

"Everyone," she replied. "The Bureau. The Kolinar delegates. The people who left. The people who never came inside at all. They are all building stories about what this is."

"And what is it?" Ardent asked.

She hesitated, then gave a small, humorless smile. "That is the problem. No one agrees."

Ardent nodded slowly. "Then we are doing something honest."

She sat beside him, her hands folded in her lap.

"The Bureau is watching more closely," she said. "They are not intervening yet, but the monitoring density has increased. Pattern analysis. Predictive modeling. Behavioral flags."

"They always do that when something resists categorization," Ardent said.

"And Kolinar?" she asked.

Ardent exhaled. "Kolinar is patient. That worries me more."

Outside the hall, a Bureau transport passed overhead, its silhouette cutting cleanly across the sky. It did not linger. It did not threaten. It simply reminded the city that observation was constant, and that neutrality was never as neutral as it pretended to be.

Across District Seven, small deviations unfolded without announcement.

A transit dispatcher paused at her console when a thought surfaced unbidden. She had followed schedules her entire adult life, measuring days in arrivals and departures. For the first time, she wondered whether direction mattered more than movement. The idea unsettled her. She dismissed it, then felt it return moments later, heavier and more insistent.

In a residential corridor three levels below the hall, a man stood in his kitchen holding a cup he had forgotten to drink from. He stared at the wall while memories rearranged themselves, not changing content, but emphasis. He could not explain why the life he had built suddenly felt provisional, as though it belonged to a draft version of himself.

A child walking home from an education center stopped and asked her parent why people existed at all. The question was met with laughter and deflection, but it followed them the rest of the way home like a shadow that refused to detach.

None of these moments were dramatic.

None were recorded.

Yet each marked a subtle deviation that no Bureau model had fully anticipated.

High above District Seven, inside the Spire, Seren Hale stood before a wall of projections that refused to stabilize.

Models conflicted. Predictions overlapped and unraveled. The clean lines of outcome probability smeared into clusters that resisted resolution. The Bureau's algorithms were built to manage deviation, not ambiguity. Humanity was no longer behaving as a single debtor. It was behaving as a divided portfolio, and the math was not designed for that.

"That should not be possible," murmured one of the analysts behind her.

Seren did not respond.

She saw the fault line clearly now. Not the one between Ardent and Deren. Not the one between the Reckoning and Kolinar. The real fracture was forming inside the Bureau itself. Some departments argued for immediate containment. Others for strategic patience. A few, quietly and dangerously, questioned whether intervention would stabilize collapse or accelerate it.

The Exchange had always preferred clean outcomes.

Humanity was becoming untidy.

Seren placed her hand against the glass and focused on the live feed of District Seven. She saw Ardent seated on the bench, posture relaxed but burdened, gaze fixed on nothing and everything at once.

He was not commanding.

He was enduring.

That, she realized, was what made him dangerous.

Back in the hall, Ardent rose from the bench and crossed the open floor toward the slab. His steps echoed softly, each one sounding louder than it should have in the stillness. He did not touch the stone. He had learned that proximity alone was enough. Meaning did not require contact. It required presence.

The Reckoning was no longer confined to symbols etched in mineral and light. It had moved outward into decisions, into divergence, into the quiet refusal of answers that arrived too easily. Ardent could feel it pressing against him now, not as obligation, but as invitation.

"We are not going to hold this together by force," he said, his voice carrying without effort. He had not intended to speak aloud, but the words felt necessary once they formed. "If this survives, it will survive because people choose it."

The woman with bright eyes stood beside him.

"Are you afraid?" she asked.

Ardent considered the question carefully. He found that he was no longer afraid in the way he once had been. Fear had softened into something steadier, something heavier.

"Yes," he said. "But not of failure."

"Of what, then?"

"Of success," Ardent replied. "Of convincing ourselves too quickly that we are right. Of mistaking agreement for truth."

Outside the hall, the city continued to breathe. Transports traced their familiar routes. Vendors called out prices. Doors opened and closed. Yet something deeper had shifted.

A subtle reorientation was underway, invisible to those who did not feel it and unavoidable to those who did.

Humanity had always believed survival was the goal.

Now it was learning that survival without authorship was merely persistence.

Some would choose safety. Some would choose meaning. Some would choose nothing at all. For the first time, those choices were no longer managed from above. They were no longer filtered through a single authority or justified by a borrowed narrative.

The weight of that freedom settled quietly across District Seven.

It did not announce itself as victory.

It announced itself as cost.

Elsewhere in the city, a Bureau liaison reviewed reports that did not align. The metrics suggested stabilization, yet the qualitative data resisted closure. Citizens were not acting out, but they were no longer acting entirely as expected. Compliance remained high. Predictability did not.

She flagged the anomaly, hesitated, then removed the flag before submitting the report. For reasons she did not examine too closely, she did not want to be the one who forced the system to choose a response too early.

In a narrow apartment overlooking the lower transit lanes, an elderly woman sat by her window and spoke softly to no one. She had lived long enough to see ideologies rise and fall, promises made and broken. Tonight, she wondered whether the ache she felt was grief or anticipation. She could not remember the last time the future had felt unsettled in a way that did not terrify her.

In another sector, a Kolinar envoy stood before a private display, reviewing the same feeds with a very different expression. Interest, not concern, shaped his posture. Humanity's fracture did not alarm him. It intrigued him. Species that divided themselves over meaning often revealed which fragments were worth cultivating.

He composed a message, then deleted it. There was time. There was always time when patience was backed by leverage.

High above, inside the Spire, Seren Hale turned away from the glass.

The room felt too quiet. The projections hummed, steady and perfect, but she no longer trusted perfection. Too often it meant that something essential had been excluded for the sake of symmetry.

She thought of Ardent standing before the slab, choosing restraint over declaration. She had expected rebellion from him. She had not expected endurance.

The Bureau could manage rebellion.

Endurance was harder to quantify.

She issued a single directive, carefully worded, designed to slow rather than stop. Observation without compression. Analysis without intervention. It was a narrow path, and she knew she would have to justify it later.

For now, she allowed herself the smallest deviation.

She hoped he would not fail.

She feared even more that he might succeed.

Back in the hall, the remaining members of the Reckoning gathered quietly. They were fewer than before. The absence of those who had left hung in the air like a missing note in a familiar melody. Yet the ones who remained felt newly visible to one another, stripped of illusion.

"We are not many," the woman with bright eyes said.

"No," Ardent agreed. "And we should not try to be."

He looked around the room, meeting each gaze in turn.

"Purpose is not a consensus," he said. "It is a commitment. It does not ask how many stand with you. It asks whether you will stand when the numbers thin."

No one argued.

No one cheered.

They nodded, slowly, unevenly, honestly.

The slab responded with a faint pulse, not brighter, but steadier. Fewer symbols glowed now, but those that remained did not flicker. They held.

Outside the hall, the night deepened. Lights along the streets of District Seven shimmered against darkening stone. Somewhere, a question surfaced in a mind that had never hosted it before. Somewhere else, a familiar belief loosened its grip.

No one tracked these moments.

No one recorded the exact instant when a life that had been drifting decided to lean toward intention.

But something did.

Far beyond Halo, in the unseen calculus of the Exchange, probabilities shifted. Threads of prediction wavered. A ledger that once categorized humanity as a manageable debtor now struggled to assign a stable classification.

One part of the species chose safety under Kolinar's shadow.

One part chose self made meaning and risk.

One part chose nothing, content to persist without asking why.

The numbers did not align as they should have.

Something like curiosity stirred in the cold machinery of cosmic judgment.

Back in the hall of unfinished thoughts, Ardent stood once more before the slab. The Reckoning gathered around him, not as followers, not as disciples, but as participants in a question that no longer belonged to any single voice.

The woman with bright eyes spoke softly. "Are we enough?"

Ardent did not look at the exit. He did not look at the dimmed symbols. He looked at the people who remained.

"We do not need to be many," he said. "Purpose does not count us. It asks whether we are willing to live by what we claim."

He placed his hand on the slab.

The stone was cool beneath his palm. The symbols pulsed once in response. Not in approval. In recognition.

"We are not a guarantee," he continued. "We are not a shield. We are not a solution."

He paused.

"We are an answer."

They met his gaze, not in perfect unison, but in honest agreement. The fracture within humanity was real now, clear and undeniable. Part of the species believed meaning should be managed by those who had already survived the test. Part believed meaning must be created, not borrowed.

Which side was right remained unwritten.

But one thing had become certain.

Whatever humanity became next would not happen by accident.

The Reckoning of why would carry the question forward.

And the universe, at last, would have to decide how to account for a species that refused to collapse into a single entry.

CHAPTER SEVENTEEN

THE PRICE OF DEFIANCE

Part One: The Quiet Undoing

The Reckoning Hall had once been a forgotten structure, a place where unused walls and abandoned architecture whispered of postponed purpose. Now it was a chamber of waking breath. The slab at its center pulsed with faint silver lines that writhed like veins beneath translucent stone. It felt alive, not because it moved, but because it listened.

Ardent Voss stood before it, hands pressed to its surface, pulse steady, gaze distant. He did not feel triumphant. He did not feel victorious. He felt something heavier, something that resembled a horizon built out of consequence and dread. The Reckoning was changing, and the world outside was beginning to feel the pressure of that change.

He closed his eyes and felt the disc beneath his skin respond to his thoughts. It pulsed once, then again, and for a moment he believed he could hear the heartbeat of the city.

When he opened his eyes, something was wrong.

The air tasted like absence. Not emptiness, but subtraction. The kind of absence that replaced things without leaving evidence they had ever been there. Conversations around him slowed. The warmth of purpose that had become the Reckoning's shared breath now felt faint and remote, like an ember trapped beneath ice.

A woman near the corner lifted her hand to speak, paused halfway, and let it fall. Not out of fear. Out of nothing.

Ardent turned toward her. "Lysa?"

She blinked, as if surprised that someone was paying attention to her existence. "I was going to say something. I do not remember why."

Her face did not show confusion. It showed disinterest. The moment had lost relevance.

Ardent felt a chill ripple across his spine. He looked at the slab again. The symbols on its surface flickered as if something were trying to erase them one by one.

"They are not stopping us," Ardent whispered.

A man beside him frowned. "Then what are they doing?"

Ardent answered slowly, each word pulled through understanding he did not want.

"They are hollowing us out."

No one had time to ask what he meant.

The world answered for him.

Part Two: Directive Two

Every public screen in Halo flickered, dimmed, and reactivated. The city's infrastructure, built to distribute information with surgical precision, now served a single voice.

Seren Hale appeared.

Her posture was as controlled as ever. Her face held no triumph, no regret, and no malice. It was the expression of someone who believed she was correcting an equation that had begun to destabilize.

"Humanity is destabilizing itself," she said. Her voice carried no emotional modulation. It did not need any. "Unauthorized purpose constructs are creating unknown variance. To preserve continuity and prevent uncertainty, Directive Two is now active."

A phrase appeared beneath her image.

DIRECTIVE TWO: REMOVE CONSEQUENCE FROM CHOICE

Most of Halo glanced at the message without interest. The words meant nothing to them yet. Their lives still moved along predictable rails, guided by the Bureau's algorithms.

To the Reckoning, it felt like a blade pressed into the core of reality.

Ardent stepped back from the slab as if something had punched through the wall of existence.

Seren continued, her voice unshaken.

"Choice becomes safe when it becomes irrelevant. Consequence is the root of suffering. Removing it prevents harm."

Her image vanished.

The screens went dark.

The world did not tremble.

It faded.

Part Three: A City Without Reasons

At first, nothing appeared to happen.

Then Halo began to forget itself.

A man approached a crosswalk. The light shifted from red to green. He paused, stared at the street as if seeing it for the first time, then turned around and walked away without purpose.

A woman at a café lifted her drink, brought it halfway to her lips, and placed it down again without expression. She stared at the cup not with confusion, but with indifference, as though the idea of consuming something no longer held consequence.

Two lovers sat face to face at a table. One began to speak. The other blinked. Their conversation dissolved mid sentence. Not because they disagreed. Because neither cared enough to continue.

A girl dropped her toy. Rather than reach for it, she tilted her head, then walked away. The toy remained on the floor, abandoned not because it was broken, but because desire itself had stopped mattering.

The streets looked the same. The people looked the same.

The intentions were gone.

Choice remained. Motion remained. But nothing followed from anything. Action no longer led anywhere. The chain between cause and effect had snapped, and no one remembered why it had ever mattered.

The city did not collapse into chaos.

It collapsed into nothing.

Part Four: The Weight of Severance

Ardent staggered as the shift took hold. His thoughts remained intact, but the thread that connected thought to motivation unraveled. He felt his breath leave him and return without urgency. His heartbeat did not quicken. Nothing inside him pointed toward the next moment.

He clutched the slab with shaking hands.

"This is not suppression," he said.

Someone behind him asked, "Then what is it?"

Ardent spoke the truth that felt like a revelation carved from agony.

"This is severance. They are removing the result from action. They are making the world unresponsive."

The woman beside him whispered, "Why would they do that?"

Ardent looked at her. Her face was already beginning to lose its emotional articulation. He grabbed her wrist, grounding her in sensation.

"Because consequence is the fuel of purpose. Without consequence, choices lose weight. Without weight, direction collapses. Without direction, there is no meaning."

The slab dimmed further.

Joran, who had once been the Reckoning's most passionate advocate, stumbled forward. His voice came soft, slow, detached.

"Purpose does not change anything. It is only a feeling."

He did not look distressed.

He looked erased.

Ardent gripped his shoulder. "Joran, speak your reason. Say it. Anchor it."

Joran stared through him.

"My reason was connection," he whispered. "Connection changes nothing."

The words fell with the finality of a door closing behind memory.

He did not lose identity.

He lost relevance.

Ardent felt something inside him break.

Joran collapsed gently to the floor, not like a man fainting, but like someone deciding there was no point in remaining upright.

CHAPTER EIGHTEEN: THE MISSING WHY

The hall held its breath.

Not the way a room grows still when something frightening happens, but in the way a body forgets the rhythm of inhaling and exhaling. The slab at the center of the Reckoning chamber pulsed weakly, as though light were leaking out of it instead of glowing from within. The symbols that once carried the weight of chosen reasons flickered, losing cohesion.

Ardent Voss stood before it, watching the drift of meaning become visible. He had never imagined that purpose could dim like a lantern in fog. It frightened him more than any Custodian from the sky ever could.

Joran sat slumped against the wall. His breathing was calm. His posture relaxed. His eyes empty. He was not unconscious and not dead, but dormant in a way that struck Ardent as fundamentally unnatural. His presence still existed, but his participation in his own existence had evaporated.

No one had screamed when it happened.

That was the most horrifying part.

Screaming requires belief that pain matters.

Directive Two had not taken pain.

It had erased the reason pain meant anything in the first place.

Ardent moved among the Reckoning, touching shoulders, whispering their chosen purposes back to them to tether their intention to memory. A few needed help forming words. Some clutched their hearts as if affirming a reason required physical effort now.

He noticed only after several minutes that one voice was absent.

Merca Lin.

He scanned the hall once, twice, a third time. She was not here.

She would never have left without telling someone.

Unless the reason to tell someone no longer mattered.

Ardent's pulse sharpened.

He approached the nearest Reckoner, a middle aged woman with silver hair threaded with streaks of violet ink from the Bureau's old identity tests. Her eyes tracked him, slower than before.

"Merca left," she said, before he could ask. "She said her head felt heavy. She needed air."

Ardent did not respond. He only moved.

He reached the entrance and stepped outside.

The air tasted wrong.

Not bitter, not polluted, not cold.

Absent.

As if the atmosphere had once carried intentions and now carried nothing but oxygen.

THE QUIET STREET

District Seven no longer resembled a place where people lived. It resembled a place where movement occurred out of habit. The difference was subtle, but devastating.

People walked, but not toward destinations.

Doors opened and closed, but no urgency moved behind them.

A woman dropped a grocery bag. Apples rolled across the sidewalk, bumping into shoes and wheels. No one bent to pick them up. Even she stared at them as though the idea of acting required a justification that no longer existed.

Ardent scanned the district with a mounting ache behind his ribs.

This was not apathy.

This was subtraction.

A world retaining mobility while losing direction.

A city that moved without traveling.

He spotted Merca near a fountain bench. Her posture was relaxed. Her clothes were neat. Her hair fell naturally over her shoulders. She looked like a person resting after a thoughtful walk.

Until he saw her eyes.

No tension lived behind them.

No spark. No yearning. No memory with weight.

"Merca," he called.

She turned. Her face lit with a pleasant smile.

"Hello, Ardent," she said.

Her tone sounded exactly like the Merca he remembered. Her mannerisms aligned. If knowledge equaled identity, she would have seemed whole.

But identity was never memory.

Identity was the connection between memory and intention.

Merca had lost that connection.

Ardent sat beside her, forcing calm into his voice.

"You left the hall. You said something felt heavy. Tell me what it was."

Merca looked thoughtfully at the fountain. She nodded as though confirming a detail in her mind.

"I remember feeling something. I remember it was important. I do not remember why."

Ardent swallowed.

"Do you want to remember?"

She blinked slowly.

"I do not want anything," she said.

Not despair.

Not melancholy.

Not numbness.

Absence.

Ardent reached for her hand. She let him take it, but there was no reason behind the gesture. No comfort. No trust. No curiosity.

Only habit.

"I remember us speaking," she continued. "I remember your voice. I remember asking questions and feeling interested. Now I remember those things, but I do not feel them."

He felt like someone watching a flame burn in a lantern only to realize the lantern had no fuel. The light was residual. It was dying. It only looked alive.

"What was your purpose?" he asked quietly.

Merca considered the question.

"I remember having one. I remember choosing it. I remember defending it. I do not remember why it mattered."

"Try to say it," Ardent urged. "Even without the why. Say the words."

She took a breath.

"My purpose was to create spaces where people could feel seen."

Her voice was clear.

Her expression empty.

Ardent whispered, "And what does that mean to you now?"

"It means nothing," Merca said, with a gentle shrug. "A thing that does not change anything does not matter. My purpose changed nothing. Therefore it has no value."

He felt something twist inside him. If purpose does not alter reality, then purpose is ornamental. Directive Two had not removed ability. It had removed effect.

Without effect, intention becomes decor.

And decor does not require belief.

"Merca," Ardent said, his voice cracking, "this is not peace. This is disconnection. You are still here, but not inside your life."

She nodded.

"Yes. That feels correct."

Ardent stood. His chest tightened until it hurt. The disc inside him pulsed like a heart that did not want to surrender.

He placed both hands on her shoulders.

"I will not let this be the end of you."

Merca smiled the softest, saddest smile possible without sadness.

"You cannot save someone who does not need saving," she said calmly. "There is nothing missing. There is nothing wrong. Everything continues."

"Continuing without reason is not living," Ardent said.

Merca did not disagree.

She also did not care.

Ardent stepped back, unable to take his eyes from her.

For the first time, he understood the true intention of Directive Two.

The Bureau was not neutralizing danger.

The Bureau was neutralizing meaning.

It was engineering continuity without consequence. A species that could operate without purpose needed no rebellion. It needed no dream. It posed no threat.

Seren Hale had not chosen cruelty.

She had chosen safety.

And safety without meaning becomes a silent extinction.

THE RETURN TO THE HALL

When Ardent re entered the Reckoning chamber, the air felt different. He had brought the absence with him. The slab flickered as though reacting to something it could not interpret.

Everyone watched him.

They sensed something had changed.

Ardent walked to the front and placed a hand on the slab. It pulsed weakly.

"They have shown us the future," he said. "It is not destruction. It is existence without purpose."

A chill rippled through the room.

He continued.

"This is worse than death. Death ends experience. This prevents experience from mattering."

Someone whispered, "Can it be reversed?"

Ardent hesitated.

That hesitation made some of them tremble.

Then the slab pulsed again.

Not faintly.

Sharply.

As if asking a question.

Ardent pressed his palm against it.

A line of symbols formed.

Not the old symbols.

New ones.

Their structure was unfamiliar. Their angles sharper. Their light colder. The Reckoning gasped.

The slab was not reacting to them.

It was responding to something outside them.

Ardent leaned closer, his voice soft.

"It is mapping what we lost."

The woman with bright eyes stepped forward. "What does that mean?"

Ardent felt the answer before he understood it.

"Purpose is not a belief," he said. "It is a force that moves reality. When it disappears, the world loses direction. When it returns, the world gains shape."

More symbols appeared. Lines connected between them. Patterns emerged.

Someone whispered, "It looks like a design."

Another whispered, "It looks alive."

Ardent whispered the truth.

"It is. Purpose is architecture. It can be built."

The room inhaled as one.

This was no longer philosophy.

This was physics.

And the slab was not a monument.

It was a blueprint.

THE FIRST REVELATION

Ardent traced one of the lines on the slab. The symbol flared beneath his touch. His chest burned where the disc rested inside him.

He felt something flow through him, not information, but orientation. A direction. A clue.

"Directive Two severed consequence," he said. "It removed the link between intention and change. Without that link, purpose collapses. But if we reconnect them, we do not restore purpose. We generate it."

A Reckoner gasped.

"Generate it how?"

Ardent turned to them, realization dawning in his eyes.

"By aligning chosen reasons into a single shared field. Individual purpose gives meaning to self. Collective purpose creates gravity. If enough reasons point toward a single direction, we create a force the Bureau cannot sever."

The slab pulsed in agreement.

Someone whispered, "This is not rebellion anymore."

Ardent nodded.

"No. This is construction. We are building something the Exchange did not anticipate. Kolinar inherited purpose. We are about to invent it."

The Reckoning stared at the slab, at the symbols that glowed brighter with every reason spoken in the room. The hall vibrated with possibility.

Not hope.

Momentum.

THE BIRTH OF THE WHY ENGINE

Ardent placed both hands on the slab. Light surged upward, filling the hall, outlining structures that were not objects, but potentials.

He saw it.

Not a machine made of wires or gears.

A machine made of belief and alignment.

A Why Engine.

Not a metaphor.

A literal generator of meaning.

Powered by chosen reasons.

Anchored by consequence.

Stabilized by direction.

Ardent stepped back as tears formed in his eyes.

"We have been trying to defend purpose," he whispered. "We have not yet begun to create it."

The room trembled.

People felt their chests lighten.

Want returned.

Choice regained weight.

The slab blazed as if resurrected.

Merca Lin remained outside, unaware that the world had begun to change again.

THE WARNING

Ardent touched the final symbol that had appeared.

The slab spoke in a voice that was not sound.

A phrase formed.

NOT ALL MEANING BELONGS TO YOU

The hall fell still.

Ardent understood.

Purpose may be generatable.

But it was not a resource without cost.

To create meaning was to claim territory in reality.

And someone already believed they owned that territory.

Kolinar.

The Exchange.

Perhaps something older.

Ardent's voice was steady.

"We fight not to remember why we exist. We fight to invent why we deserve to."

The Reckoning did not cheer.

They understood.

They were no longer preserving humanity.

They were redefining it.

And far beyond Halo, something shifted in the dark like a predator scenting a rival.

Humanity had built its first tool of purpose.

The universe had noticed.

CHAPTER NINETEEN

THE CONTEST OF VOICES

Night did not fall over District Seven. It receded. Light slipped away not because the sun set, but because illumination lost the will to continue. Shadows lengthened without cause. Lamps flickered without failure. The sky hesitated between brightness and nothing, uncertain whether existence still required contrast.

People wandered out of habit rather than destination. Their steps made no sound of purpose. Their movements carried no tension of desire. They were not calm. They were incomplete.

Something waited above the city.

Ardent Voss stood at the center of the plaza before the Reckoning hall, the slab of obsidian behind him pulsing faintly like a watchful heart. The Reckoning had formed a loose circle around him. Their faces were taut with something more precise than fear.

Expectation.

The disc inside Ardent's chest pulsed once. Not a warning. A summons.

The world inhaled without knowing why.

The sky trembled.

Then it spoke.

THE FIRST VOICE

A voice appeared without origin. It did not descend from the heavens or rise from the earth. It did not echo. It existed.

"Humanity has created intention without permission."

A ripple passed over every mind. Some clutched their heads. Others widened their eyes. Children paused mid laugh, bewildered by the sudden absence of laughter's purpose.

Ardent knew the voice.

The Exchange.

Its tone held no emotion and no malice. It was the balance sheet of reality reading itself aloud.

"Meaning destabilizes without debt. Purpose unmeasured is trespass."

The words did not intimidate. They defined.

Ardent stepped forward. He did not shout. He did not plead.

"We did not trespass. We remembered."

Silence answered him. The kind of silence that was not empty, but listening.

Then a second voice appeared. Harder. Older. Sharper. Not judging, but measuring.

"Memory is not qualification."

Light lanced across the sky, bending into shape. It resembled a figure only because human minds required form to hold meaning.

Kolinar had arrived.

Its body shimmered, clothed in fractal light that never settled into certainty. Its eyes were not windows. They were verdicts.

Kolinar spoke.

"Purpose belongs to those who survived the Contest. Humanity was not chosen. You were spared. You were allowed. You were supervised. You do not own meaning."

Gasps scattered across the plaza as if fear had been waiting to be invited.

Ardent answered.

"We are not asking for ownership. We are choosing existence that matters."

Kolinar's form brightened. Light folded inward, like a thought constricting.

"Existence without inheritance is chaos. You invent meaning like sparks from flint. Every spark risks a fire."

Ardent did not flinch.

"Perhaps a fire was always necessary."

Kolinar tilted its head. The gesture conveyed confusion without emotion.

"You confuse necessity with novelty. You think invention is creation. Meaning is not new. Meaning is earned."

The slab behind Ardent pulsed, as if recognizing a wound opening.

Ardent did not respond.

Because a third voice had entered the night.

THE WITNESS ARRIVES

"I observe."

It did not sound like a declaration. It sounded like the beginning of a story.

Space shimmered. Not rupture. Recognition. The Advocate unfolded into existence, not as form, but as orientation. It did not look like anything. It felt like acknowledgment.

The Advocate spoke.

"I do not assign. I do not command. I do not inherit. I witness what becomes possible."

Ardent felt the disc in his chest respond, as if some internal resonance had identified kinship.

The Advocate was not power.

The Advocate was consequence.

Kolinar's light hardened.

"Your presence invites deviation."

The Advocate replied.

"Deviation reveals direction."

The Exchange entered again.

"Direction without structure is violation."

Ardent lifted his chin.

"Structure without choice is captivity."

The statement vibrated across the plaza. Lights flickered. Hearts quickened. Not in fear. In alignment.

Three forces now converged:

The Exchange, which balanced existence.

Kolinar, which guarded inherited purpose.

The Advocate, which observed potential.

And humanity, which dared to invent meaning.

The Contest had begun.

THE EXCHANGE MAKES ITS CLAIM

Symbols, vast as constellations, appeared across the sky. Each one thrummed like a law beyond language.

"Meaning requires debt."

"Debt requires recognition."

"Recognition requires lineage."

"Humanity has no lineage."

The Exchange paused, then delivered the verdict.

"Humanity violates equilibrium."

Ardent stepped forward.

"Humanity restores possibility."

The Exchange replied instantly.

"Possibility destabilizes. You introduce variance without collateral. You generate purpose without permission. You risk collapse beyond your species."

Some citizens trembled. Others straightened.

Fear and awakening often arrive in the same breath.

Ardent inhaled slowly.

"Meaning without permission is not risk. It is freedom."

The Exchange allowed the words to exist without answering them.

Which was its answer.

KOLINAR CLAIMS THE THRONE

Kolinar descended. Not closer. More present. Its presence pressed into perception like gravity acquiring mass.

"Meaning requires anchor. Your species has no anchor. You invent reasons without substance. You disrupt order without offering replacement."

Ardent replied.

"Our meaning is not inheritance. It is invention."

Kolinar's light tightened.

"Invention is arrogance. You do not understand the weight of purpose. You have not faced the cost. You have not endured the Contest. You are children claiming crowns forged from catastrophe. You seek to shape reality without surviving it."

The Reckoning wavered. Some eyes flickered with doubt.

Ardent felt it like a pressure on his chest.

Doubt was not failure.

Doubt was price.

He answered.

"If meaning requires inheritance, it is not meaning. It is inheritance. We refuse to inherit. We choose to create."

Kolinar shifted, light fracturing along invisible axes.

"Choice is irrelevant without consequence. You do not comprehend the cost of why."

Ardent whispered.

"We do now."

The plaza quieted. The slab behind him pulsed once, faint but resolute.

Kolinar paused.

The pause was not silence.

The pause was fear.

Not of humanity.

Of what humanity might become.

THE ADVOCATE SETS THE TERMS

The Advocate spoke again, gentle as gravity.

"Three claims seek authority."

Symbols formed in the air, enormous and unignorable.

The Exchange claims meaning requires debt.

Kolinar claims meaning requires inheritance.

Humanity claims meaning requires choice.

A fourth sentence appeared.

Only one structure can govern a species.

Ardent felt his stomach tighten. This was not philosophy. This was designation.

Rights were not ideas.

Rights were architectures.

The Advocate continued.

"Humanity must select one or create one."

Gasps burst around him. People shook their heads as if the motion could erase the implications.

Ardent felt the disc burn in his chest.

He spoke.

"We choose creation."

The Advocate asked.

"Can you defend what you create?"

Ardent answered without hesitation.

"We can."

Kolinar's form expanded.

"Then speak."

Ardent blinked.

"What?"

Kolinar replied.

"You invented meaning. Declare it. Present it. The Contest has begun."

The Exchange added.

"One cycle remains."

The Advocate clarified.

"If the reason stands, humanity evolves. If it fails, humanity continues without why."

The words landed like meteors.

Humanity was not threatened with death.

Humanity was threatened with continuance without purpose.

The universe was not choosing whether humanity lived.

It was choosing whether humanity mattered.

THE CROWD DIVIDES

The plaza erupted, not into chaos, but into voices. Some shouted support. Others cried out in fear. Some turned away, unwilling to risk a life with cost.

A woman near the front lifted her child.

"I want her to live with reason," she whispered.

A man beside her shook his head.

"Reason invites burden. Burden invites conflict. We should remain safe."

Clusters formed.

Lines appeared.

Not physical boundaries.

Philosophical ones.

Ardent watched the fracture widen. He recognized it.

This was not destruction.

This was separation into identities.

The first step in specieshood.

The Reckoning held their place, eyes fierce, posture steady. Their voices carried quiet certainty.

"We choose meaning."

Kolinar observed them.

"You choose suffering."

Ardent shook his head.

"Suffering without reason is torment. Suffering with purpose is transformation."

The Exchange responded.

"Transformation is risk."

Ardent replied.

"Without risk, there is no humanity."

SEREN HALE WATCHES

Far above the plaza, in the Spire, Seren Hale stood on the observation floor. The screens around her displayed every angle of the gathering.

Her posture remained composed, but something inside her cracked like ice under heat.

Her subordinate, Jalen Rhyse, stood beside her. His voice shook.

"They are dividing. Humanity is fracturing."

Seren did not blink.

"Humanity was never unified. We only prevented expression."

Jalen swallowed.

"We can still end this."

She did not answer immediately.

When she did, her voice was quiet.

"End what? Choice?"

Jalen hesitated.

"Choice leads to suffering."

Seren closed her eyes.

"So does purpose."

Jalen whispered.

"You sound uncertain."

Seren whispered back.

"I sound human."

The screens flickered.

Something outside the Bureau's understanding was taking shape.

THE FIRST HUMAN RESPONSE

Ardent stepped onto the slab. Its symbols flared beneath him, recognizing intention.

He lifted his voice. Not loud. Not forced.

Certain.

"Humanity exists to create meaning where none is given."

The words struck reality like a key fitting a lock.

The Exchange faltered. Kolinar's form distorted. The Advocate watched, still as a horizon.

Ardent continued.

"Meaning is not debt. Meaning is not inheritance. Meaning is creation. We do not exist because the universe recognized us. We exist because we recognize ourselves."

A murmur spread through the plaza.

Recognition.

Humanity had never asked permission to be.

It had asked only for the courage to believe it was worth existing.

Ardent finished.

"We claim purpose because we choose purpose. Choice is not violation. Choice is existence."

The slab blazed bright enough to light the plaza. A pulse ran through the ground.

The Contest of Voices shifted.

Not away from humanity.

Toward it.

THE FIRST VERDICT

The Exchange spoke first.

"Recognition pending."

Kolinar's light narrowed.

"Demand proof."

The Advocate delivered the sentence.

"One cycle remains. Present your reason as structure. Not as voice. Not as wish. As architecture."

Ardent understood.

This was not debate.

This was construction.

They had one cycle to build meaning that could survive examination.

Not metaphor.

Mechanism.

The Why Engine had to be completed.

The plaza quieted as the forces withdrew. The sky sealed itself like a courtroom door closing.

The Reckoning turned to Ardent, eyes filled with fear and ignition.

"What do we do now?" someone whispered.

Ardent answered.

"We build."

THE WORLD BREATHES

The crowd dispersed, not slowly, not quickly, but with direction. The air no longer drifted. It moved. People walked not because walking was habit, but because distance mattered again. Choices regained consequence. The city woke like a sleeper remembering dreams.

Ardent remained in the plaza until the last light faded. He stood alone, breathing the air that tasted like potential.

The disc in his chest pulsed once more, like a heartbeat synchronizing with something larger.

Not fear.

Responsibility.

He whispered to the empty sky.

"This is not a punishment."

Then his voice hardened.

"This is an invitation."

And somewhere in the silent spaces between stars, something answered.

Not with words.

With attention.

Humanity was no longer a species.

It was a contestant. And the universe was watching.

CHAPTER TWENTY

THE DEADLINE

The plaza did not settle after the voices departed. It held tension like a lung that refused to exhale. People remained where they stood, afraid to move not because motion was dangerous, but because motion implied decision, and decision suddenly mattered more than it ever had before.

Ardent Voss did not speak at first. His breathing was steady, but his pulse carried the tremor of a man who had realized that time was no longer a passive condition. It was now a weapon aimed at the soul of his species.

The Advocate's final words reverberated through the plaza, not as sound, but as structure.

One cycle.

Not a measure of hours. Not a season. A span of existence calibrated to meaning. The Exchange had granted humanity an interval. Within it, they must prove their right to purpose. Time itself had become conditional.

Ardent faced the Reckoning. Their eyes were wide, their posture frozen between readiness and disbelief. No one knew how to begin. They only understood that beginning was mandatory.

A voice broke the silence.

"What happens at the end of the cycle?"

The question did not belong to a single person. It belonged to humanity itself. Every face leaned toward Ardent as if waiting for the definition of fate.

Ardent turned slowly, meeting their gaze one by one.

"We answer. Or we do not."

The woman with bright eyes stepped forward. Her voice quivered like something fragile struggling not to break.

"And if we fail?"

Ardent hesitated, not for lack of knowledge, but for precision. Words were no longer descriptions. They were architecture.

"If we fail, humanity continues without purpose. Our bodies will live. Our species will endure. But we will not dream. We will not desire. We will not care. We will walk through existence as if it were a corridor with no doors, no exits, and no discovery. We will survive because survival requires no meaning. We will no longer be human because humanity requires a why."

A murmur rose, soft as dust lifting from stone.

Someone asked, "So extinction is not the threat?"

Ardent shook his head.

"Extinction ends suffering. Meaninglessness does not. It continues endlessly because there is nothing left inside capable of wanting it to end."

The silence that followed felt heavier than fear. It was the silence of comprehension.

Humanity had always feared death.

Now it understood there was something infinitely worse.

Survival without purpose.

THE BUREAU RESPONDS

Screens throughout the district shuddered awake. Seren Hale appeared, framed by the Bureau's insignia. Her shoulders were squared. Her expression was smooth. Her hair was arranged with meticulous precision. Her voice cut through the stillness like protocol.

"Directive Two remains in effect. Unauthorized purpose constructs threaten continuity. Meaning is volatile. Choice without regulation destabilizes the species. We must preserve equilibrium."

Her tone held no emotion. It held conclusion.

"The Audit approaches. Failure cannot be allowed. Humanity must survive. Therefore, humanity must be unburdened. We will remove whatever disrupts continuity."

Ardent felt his chest tighten. Seren's words were not threats. They were promises spoken in the language of inevitability.

Survival without uncertainty was survival without choice. Survival without choice was survival without reason. Survival without reason was the quiet death that had consumed Merca Lin.

Seren Hale believed she was saving humanity.

She was amputating its soul.

The broadcast continued.

"Any attempt to create or disseminate purpose outside Bureau authorization will be considered hostile action. We will protect humanity from collapse."

Her image faded.

The plaza did not erupt. It sagged.

One of the Reckoning whispered, "They think they are helping."

Ardent replied, "The most dangerous prisons are built by those who believe they are protecting us from ourselves. They do not know they are removing the thing that makes us alive."

THE UNBURDENED

Not everyone recoiled from the Bureau's message.

Some welcomed it.

A small group stepped forward, faces serene, movements unhurried. Their voices rose together. They did not chant. They confessed.

"Meaning is pain. Purpose is conflict. Direction is weight. We choose quiet. We choose rest. We choose the end of wanting."

Their tone did not accuse. It invited.

A woman in the Reckoning recoiled. "They have given up."

Ardent watched carefully.

"They have not surrendered to despair. They have surrendered to relief. To some, meaning feels like drowning. They would rather float in emptiness than struggle through purpose."

The Unburdened closed their eyes. Their lips curved in soft, harmless smiles.

They were not a mob.

They were gravity pulling downward on the human spirit.

The threat was not violence.

It was resignation.

THE DEADLINE MANIFESTS

The sky flickered. Clouds parted without wind. A line of text formed in letters of light that did not shine outward, but inward.

ONE CYCLE TO PRESENT HUMANITY'S REASON

Another line appeared beneath it.

FAILURE RESULTS IN CONTINUATION WITHOUT PURPOSE

A final sentence carved itself across the heavens.

CARE OR CEASE TO CARE

Some screamed. Others fell to their knees. A few stared straight ahead, hollowed out by the weight of comprehension.

The universe had distilled humanity's future into a choice that was not binary.

It was singular.

Ardent stepped forward. His voice shook only once before it found its footing.

"The Exchange has given us a deadline. Kolinar has given us a warning. The Bureau has given us a future without direction. We have one task."

He placed his hand over his heart. The disc pulsed beneath his palm as if answering a call it had been waiting for since the first question was asked.

"Find a reason worth existence. Not a belief. Not a preference. A purpose strong enough to withstand scrutiny. A purpose that does not collapse in silence."

The slab inside the Reckoning hall flickered, as if responding to his declaration.

Ardent continued.

"We do this not because the Exchange demands it. We do this because without purpose we are not a species. We are inventory."

His voice sharpened.

"One cycle begins now."

No one moved. No one spoke.

The city had become a courtroom waiting for a verdict that had not been written.

Ardent turned away and walked back into the hall. The Reckoning followed, not because they understood the path, but because there was no other one left.

THE FIRST FAILURE

Inside the hall, Merca Lin sat against the wall. She blinked once every few seconds. Her posture was relaxed. Her eyes were alive.

Her why was gone.

Ardent knelt beside her.

"Merca. Do you remember?"

She nodded. "I remember everything. I remember caring. I do not care now. It is peaceful."

Ardent felt the wound reopen.

"Would you take that peace back if you could feel meaning again?"

Merca smiled, not cruelly, but gently.

"Why would I want the weight of wanting?"

Her answer struck Ardent harder than any opposition he had faced.

Purpose was not merely a prize.

Purpose was work.

And not everyone desired it.

The Reckoning watched in silence, unable to decide which was more terrifying.

A world without purpose.

Or a world that offered it, and found that some preferred to live without it.

INSIDE THE BUREAU

Far above the district, Seren Hale paced at the apex of the Spire. Surveillance streams flowed around her like a constellation of screens. Jalen Rhyse stood at her side.

"Public division is increasing," Jalen reported.

Seren did not look at him. "Division is natural. Division is manageable. What matters is that they cannot organize."

Jalen hesitated. "But what if they do?"

Seren paused. Her voice dropped to a murmur.

"Humanity creates reasons to fight. Reasons to die. Reasons to destroy. If we eliminate reasons, we eliminate conflict."

Jalen whispered, "And creation?"

Seren closed her eyes.

"Creation is the root of danger."

Her calm had cracks. Each crack was a pulse of memory.

Her night with Ardent.

Her belief that connection was necessary.

The ache she thought was weakness.

The longing she had tried to regulate.

She had once wanted something.

Want was unstable.

Want was unpredictable.

Want was alive.

She would not let herself feel it again.

THE DISC IN ARDENT'S CHEST

Back in the hall, Ardent stood over the slab. His chest burned.

The disc pulsed in a rhythm that felt older than choice. Its glow reflected in the slab, causing symbols to shimmer and align in shapes no one recognized.

The Reckoning watched him.

"What is happening to you?" someone asked.

Ardent placed his hand against the stone.

"I think this is what choice feels like when reality notices."

A tremor passed through the hall. The symbols rearranged. A pattern emerged, faint but deliberate.

The Why Engine.

It had begun.

Not as a machine.

As a structure.

The Reckoning held their breath as Ardent spoke.

"Meaning must be built. Not claimed. Not inherited. Built."

The slab brightened.

Purpose was not an answer.

Purpose was construction.

A NEW FACTION

A voice called from the doorway.

"I know what purpose is."

Everyone turned.

Deren Sol reentered the hall. Behind him stood those who had left with him, bearing expressions neither empty nor loyal.

"We have spoken with Kolinar. We have seen what inheritance offers. It is structure. It is safety. It is certainty."

He pointed at Ardent.

"You offer struggle without guarantee. Hope without direction. Meaning without anchor. You risk everything for a why that has no blueprint."

Ardent replied.

"Meaning requires risk. Without it, purpose is obedience."

Deren stepped closer.

"And what if obedience is better than oblivion?"

The question struck the hall like a fault line opening.

The Reckoning divided into three camps:

Those who believed purpose required risk.

Those who believed purpose required inheritance.

Those who believed purpose required nothing at all.

Humanity was fracturing faster than time allowed.

THE HOUR THAT WAS NOT AN HOUR

The Advocate's voice echoed without form.

"Cycle initiated."

Lights flickered. The disc in Ardent's chest flared.

The Why Engine shimmered into view. Not complete. Not ready. Not enough.

Ardent whispered to the Reckoning.

"We are not trying to prove we deserve to live. We are proving we deserve to matter."

No one dared answer.

Not because they disagreed.

Because they understood.

To matter was heavier than survival.

To matter demanded cost.

Ardent looked at the slab. Its symbols pulsed faintly, like stars not yet born.

He placed his hand upon it.

"We begin now."

The hall filled with breath.

The world beyond held its own.

The cycle had started, not with movement, but with awakening.

The deadline was not a clock.

The deadline was the question:

Will humanity care?

Or cease to?

CHAPTER TWENTY-ONE

THE RECKONING RESPONDS

The hall felt different.

The walls had not shifted. The ceiling had not lowered. The slab still stood at the center like a dark planet suspended in the orbit of human attention. Yet something had changed in the air itself. It was thicker. Heavier. Every breath carried weight.

The Reckoning understood why.

They were no longer an idea. They were an obligation.

Ardent Voss stood in front of the slab. The obsidian surface pulsed with faint light beneath his fingers, a weak but persistent heartbeat. The symbols carved into it shimmered in and out of focus, as if the stone itself waited to decide whether it believed in them.

No one spoke at first.

The silence was not empty. It was crowded with pressure. Words had always mattered, but now they could alter the fate of a species. Every sentence, every reason, every chosen purpose had become a structural element in something larger than any of them.

Ardent drew in a careful breath. The disc in his chest pulsed in rhythm with the slab, as if he were not simply standing in front of meaning, but connected to it.

His voice, when he finally spoke, was steady. It carried something new.

Responsibility.

"We are not here to write a rule," he said. "We are not here to choose a single reason that humanity must repeat. We are not here to force belief."

He placed his right hand on the slab. The symbols brightened slightly, as though listening.

"We are here to find out whether humanity deserves meaning at all."

The words landed heavily. There was no murmur, no scattered reaction. Only a deeper quiet, like the soundlessness beneath a deep ocean.

The slab pulsed once.

A young man near the front swallowed and stepped forward. His hands trembled, but his eyes did not.

"I believe humanity exists to create what did not exist before," he said. "Not only objects. Possibilities."

The slab flared with a thin line of light that ran along its surface.

Someone else found courage in that spark.

"I believe we exist to turn confusion into understanding," a woman said. "To transform chaos into pattern. Experience into memory."

A second line joined the first.

A third voice came, rough and unsure, but honest.

"I believe we exist to love. Even though it hurts. Especially because it hurts. Nothing else reaches so far beyond us."

The light spread.

It did not form words. It formed pathways.

More voices joined, some firm and clear, others broken and hesitant.

"I exist to defy what tells me I am nothing."

"I exist to take pain and give it meaning."

"I exist to plant something where there was emptiness."

"I exist to witness other lives and say they mattered."

"I exist because someone needs to remember that we can be better than we were yesterday."

"I exist to ask questions that have no answers, because the asking changes me."

Each reason struck the slab like the impact of a hammer on metal. Symbols stirred. Patterns throbbed. The surface of the stone looked less like decoration and more like circuitry that was beginning to carry current.

The Reckoning was not reciting doctrine.

They were giving shape to a field.

Ardent raised his hand and they fell quiet.

"The Exchange wants one reason," he said.

He let that hang in the air.

"That is the trap."

The hall focused on him so intensely he felt their attention like warmth against his skin.

"If humanity offers one reason, then one group will own it. One idea will become law. One vision will suppress all others. That is not meaning. That is a cage."

He stepped closer to the slab. Its glow washed over his face.

"Meaning is not a sentence. It is a direction. A shared direction does not require us to share the same words. It requires us to move toward the same horizon."

A woman in the second row nodded slowly.

"So we are not searching for one answer," she said. "We are constructing one momentum."

Ardent allowed himself a brief, tired smile.

"Exactly. The Exchange measures stability. Kolinar measures inheritance. We measure choice. Our reason is not a phrase. Our reason is that we choose to have one."

The slab erupted with light. Not a blinding flash, but a steady expansion. Symbols shifted into new arrangements, no longer scattered fragments, but connected arcs, overlapping loops, intersecting angles. The pattern did not resolve into a single message.

It resolved into a position.

The Reckoning leaned forward as if the future had just stepped one pace closer to them.

Ardent turned back to face them.

"Our task is not to agree on a single purpose," he said. "Our task is to prove that purpose itself is part of what humanity is. Not granted. Not imposed. Created."

He gestured to the slab.

"This is not a monument. It is a record. It holds the reasons we have already spoken. It will hold more. It will change as we change. That is not a weakness. That is proof that it belongs to us."

The woman with bright eyes stepped closer, her gaze drawn by the shifting light.

"How do we present something that is not a sentence?" she asked. "The Exchange expects a statement. A claim. A declaration."

Ardent did not hesitate.

"By living it."

A hush swept through the room like a tide.

He continued.

"We show the universe a species that refuses emptiness. A species that takes meaningless existence and carves value into it. A species that looks at a blank page and decides that the page does not win."

The slab pulsed in rhythm with his words, as though the idea itself had begun to anchor in something beneath the physical.

Then the doors opened.

Two figures stepped inside.

They had once stood with Deren Sol.

THE RETURN OF THE DOUBTFUL

Their faces were pale. Their eyes were wide, not with fanatic devotion and not with emptiness, but with the shock of people who have witnessed something they cannot ignore.

Everyone turned.

One of them, a thin man with short dark hair and a scar along his left jaw, spoke first.

"They have begun," he said.

Ardent felt tension coil in his stomach.

"Who," he asked, "and what have they begun?"

"The Unburdened," the man answered. "They are growing. They are moving through the districts. They are telling people that peace lies in not caring. That the deadline is a lie. Or worse, that it is real but irrelevant."

The second, a woman with cropped silver hair and deep lines around her mouth, stepped forward.

"They offer three promises," she said quietly. "First, that if you surrender purpose, you will never suffer again. Second, that if you stop asking why, nothing can disappoint you. Third, that if you give up, the Bureau will protect you and life will go on."

Her tone was not mocking.

It was afraid.

Ardent looked around the hall.

The Reckoning did not gasp. They did not cry out.

They sank inward, each person suddenly aware that their opponent was not only cosmic and not only institutional.

It was human.

The woman with bright eyes whispered, "Some people will want that. They are exhausted. They are afraid. They are angry that meaning hurts."

Ardent nodded.

"They are not cowards," he said. "They are tired. They have been promised too many hollow reasons. They are not rejecting purpose. They are rejecting disappointment."

The man who had spoken first added, "The Unburdened say the Reckoning is cruel. They say you are asking people to carry what they should never have been given. They say meaning is the disease, not the cure."

A long, slow breath moved across the hall.

The Reckoning had thought their struggle was against the Bureau and against the Exchange and against Kolinar.

Now they understood that part of that struggle would be against the part of humanity that yearned for sleep.

FIELD TEST

Ardent moved his hand across the slab. The symbols shifted, responding to his unresolved thought. New arcs appeared. A segment on the right side of the stone flared and dimmed like an unsteady flame.

"We need to know what the Why Engine can do," he said. "Not in theory. In lives."

He pointed to a small side chamber that had once been used for storage and now held chairs, cushions, and a few scattered artifacts from earlier gatherings.

"Bring someone in here. Someone who is close to giving up. Someone who still remembers they used to care."

A few Reckoners exchanged glances. Then one of them, a younger woman with ink stains on her fingers from years of Bureau record work, nodded.

"I know someone," she said. "My brother. He was curious once. He is listening to the Unburdened now."

"Bring him," Ardent said.

She left.

The hall waited.

The slab pulsed, as if restless.

Ardent used the time to outline what little he understood.

"The Why Engine is not a device we switch on," he said. "It is a field we nourish. Each reason you speak adds structure. Each act you take in alignment with that reason adds stability."

He looked at them all.

"Understand this. Purpose is not a shield. It is a lens. It does not prevent pain. It changes what pain becomes."

Some nodded slowly.

Others did not.

They did not argue. They simply carried their doubts more openly now.

After several minutes, the ink stained woman returned, guiding a man in his mid twenties. His shoulders slumped. His eyes flicked briefly around the hall and then settled into a distant stare that said, clearly, that he expected nothing.

"This is Liren," she said. "My brother."

Liren gave a small nod. It felt less like greeting and more like compliance.

Ardent approached him gently.

"Do you know why you are here?" he asked.

Liren shrugged.

"My sister believes you can make caring hurt less," he said.

"Can you?" Ardent asked.

Liren surprised him with a small, humorless smile.

"If you can, I will believe in you."

Ardent did not return the smile.

"I cannot make caring hurt less," he said. "But I may be able to help you understand why it should hurt at all."

He led Liren closer to the slab.

The stone flared softly in their presence.

Ardent spoke to the room.

"We are going to try something. We are not going to tell Liren what to believe. We are going to build a space around him made of reasons and see whether that gives him back the right to want anything."

He placed one hand on Liren's shoulder and the other on the slab.

"Those of you who are willing," Ardent said, "speak your reasons. Not at him. Around him."

A voice arose from the left.

"I exist to turn loneliness into connection."

Another from the back.

"I exist to notice what others ignore."

A third, trembling but resolute.

"I exist to turn regret into promise."

The reasons continued, filling the hall with quiet declarations.

"I exist so that my child will know that life is more than survival."

"I exist to tell stories that keep others from disappearing."

"I exist to change how suffering is remembered."

Liren stood with his eyes closed, seemingly unaffected.

Then his breathing changed.

It deepened.

His shoulders straightened slightly, as if some weight had shifted, not away, but into a position he could carry.

Ardent watched the slab.

Symbols aligned around Liren's position like a constellation forming a new pattern. Light flowed along specific channels, outlining the space around him. Not a prison. Not a shield.

A context.

"Tell me what you feel," Ardent said.

Liren opened his eyes slowly.

"It still hurts," he said. "But it is not pointless. The hurt sits somewhere now. It does not float."

A subtle exhale rippled through the room.

Ardent nodded.

"That is the beginning," he said softly. "Purpose does not always reduce pain. Sometimes it gives pain a location inside meaning. That is enough to keep someone from falling through themselves."

Liren turned his gaze toward the slab.

"What is this thing?" he asked.

Ardent looked at the glowing stone.

"This," he said, "is us. Or it is becoming us."

Liren frowned.

"And the Unburdened?"

Ardent answered with care.

"They offer sleep. We offer a difficult morning. The difference is that after morning, there is a day."

Liren considered that.

"Can I leave if I still want sleep?" he asked.

"Yes," Ardent said immediately. "Purpose chosen under pressure is control. Purpose chosen freely is creation."

Liren nodded once.

"I will stay for now," he said. "It helps that you allowed the option to leave."

He stepped back into the crowd, no longer empty, not fully awakened, but attached again to his own life by a fragile thread.

The Reckoning watched him as if watching their first small victory.

They had not converted him.

They had not erased his fear.

They had given his fear a place to stand.

The Why Engine glowed more steadily now.

SEREN HALE REMEMBERS

In the Spire, Seren Hale stared at her reflection in the observation window. The city stretched beneath her, divided between light and shadow.

Jalen Rhyse stood behind her, the data projection hovering between them.

"Directive Two had partial failure in District Seven," he reported. "Purpose constructs resisted full severance. The individuals associated with the Reckoning are creating reinforcement phenomena. We do not understand the mechanism."

Seren closed her eyes.

"It is not a mechanism," she said. "It is a decision."

Jalen frowned.

"They are destabilizing the population. They are creating hope."

Seren's jaw tightened.

"Hope is leverage. It invites risk. Risk invites collapse."

Jalen tried again.

"If they succeed, humanity might pass the Contest on its own terms."

Seren turned sharply.

"And if they fail, every person who believed in them will experience not only suffering, but the knowledge that suffering meant nothing. The fall from false meaning is more destructive than never having believed at all."

Her voice softened.

"I will not let humanity experience that fall."

She did not say, aloud, that she had once fallen in her own way.

She had once allowed herself to believe that connection mattered. That one night, one touch, one admission of desire, could live inside a life built on discipline.

She had been wrong.

She had buried that part of herself for the sake of what she called duty.

Now the universe itself had resurrected it in the form of a species asking why.

"We proceed," she said. "Directive Two holds. We will apply more precise interventions. We will let the Reckoning pull as hard as they can. When they fail, the collapse will prove that we were always right."

Jalen stared at her.

"And if they do not fail?" he asked.

Seren answered without moving.

"Then they will have done what I could not."

THE COST OF CARING

Back in the hall, the Reckoning settled after Liren's small transformation. No one clapped. No one celebrated. They had seen enough to understand that this was not triumph.

It was proof of concept.

Babies do not win wars.

They prove that a future is still possible.

Ardent turned again to the slab.

"It is not enough to demonstrate this to ourselves," he said. "The Exchange does not watch what we claim. It watches what we become."

The woman with bright eyes nodded.

"We must live our reasons in a way that can be witnessed."

Another Reckoner spoke.

"But how can the universe measure something as intimate as why?"

Ardent thought of the Advocate.

"It does not measure the words," he said. "It measures the changes those words cause."

He walked slowly around the slab, touching its edge as if using it to steady his thoughts.

"If we say we exist to create possibility, then the world around us must hold more possibility. If we say we exist to transform suffering, then there must be suffering that is transformed. If we say we exist to love, then some lives must be altered by love."

He stopped.

"Our reasons are not poetry. They are contracts with reality. If we speak them and nothing changes, then we have lied."

The hall absorbed that truth with a mixture of awe and dread.

The young man who had spoken first earlier raised his voice again.

"Then caring is dangerous," he said softly. "Because once we claim a purpose, the universe will hold us to it."

Ardent nodded slowly.

"Yes," he said. "That is what makes it real."

THE RECKONING BECOMES A SIGNAL

The slab brightened, its symbols expanding into a glowing lattice that reached beyond the edges of the stone like light trying to remember how to become a constellation.

Thin threads of luminescence extended upward, vanishing into air that no longer felt entirely empty.

The disc in Ardent's chest pulsed harder, pulling his breath out of rhythm for a moment.

He understood, then.

The Why Engine was no longer just inside the hall.

It was sending something out.

Not a message. Not words.

A pattern.

A field of directed choice.

"We are broadcasting," Ardent murmured. "Not to convince. To reveal."

"Reveal what?" someone asked.

"That there is a species that chooses to care," he answered.

He imagined the Advocate watching. He imagined Kolinar feeling the disturbance, unsettled that meaning might not be confined to its domain. He imagined the Exchange recalculating, uneasy that a new variable had arrived that did not originate from any ledger.

He also imagined the Unburdened, closing their eyes tighter, pressing their minds against the offer of purpose and refusing it like a light that hurt their eyes.

Care was becoming a signal.

It would draw allies.

It would draw enemies.

It would draw cost.

Ardent looked over the Reckoning.

"There is something we must accept now," he said. "If we succeed, we will not only justify humanity's right to meaning. We will change the rules for every species that has ever inherited purpose instead of choosing it."

The woman with bright eyes whispered, "We are not only risking ourselves."

Ardent met her gaze.

"True," he said. "But the rules have already harmed us. Perhaps it is time they answer to someone."

THE DECLARATION

The hall quieted again. The slab's light steadied. The patterns on its surface did not resolve into a final design. They remained open, inviting.

The Reckoning stood ready.

Ardent placed both hands on the stone.

"We are not the whole of humanity," he said. "We do not claim to speak for everyone. Some will choose Kolinar. Some will choose the Bureau. Some will choose the Unburdened. We will not take away their choice."

He drew in a slow breath.

"But we will offer something else. We will present a species that contains at least one group that refuses emptiness. That sees existence without meaning as a wound and chooses to bleed rather than accept it."

His voice deepened.

"We do not fight to survive. Survival belongs to biology. We fight because we care. We fight because caring hurts. And we fight because, in spite of that hurt, we would rather feel everything than feel nothing."

The slab responded.

Its symbols aligned into a radiant pattern that was still incomplete, but now undeniably coherent. The Why Engine hummed in a pitch that no ear could fully hear but every heart could feel.

The Reckoning straightened.

They were no longer an idea.

They were a response.

A declaration.

A direction.

Somewhere beyond the horizon of Halo, in realms humanity had never seen, the Exchange adjusted its equations. Kolinar tightened its hold on inherited meaning. The Advocate leaned closer, not with affection, but with interest.

For the first time since the Contest was announced, the universe had something new to consider.

A species that did not inherit purpose.

A species that refused to surrender it.

A species that chose it.

Humanity had not yet proven its why.

But in the echoing heart of the hall, in the glow of the living stone, in the tremor of gathered voices refusing silence, something had become true.

The Reckoning had responded.

Now the universe would decide what that answer was worth.

CHAPTER TWENTY-TWO

THE COST OF MEANING

The Reckoning did not sleep.

Some lay down on the floor with their eyes open, staring at the ceiling as if it might begin to answer questions back. Others sat in clusters, knees drawn up, speaking in low voices that never quite settled into conversation. Words drifted through the hall that sounded less like planning and more like people trying to keep their minds from floating away.

They were not afraid of the dark.

They were afraid of drifting.

The slab at the center of the room glowed with patterns that no longer looked like scattered marks. Lines of light wove through one another, forming arcs and junctions that resembled a map drawn over a territory that did not yet fully exist. The symbols pulsed, not with random energy, but with something rhythmic and insistent.

Meaning.

It had taken shape.

And because Ardent Voss understood the nature of reality now, he knew what that meant.

Real things require cost.

He stood a little apart from the others, arms folded loosely, gaze fixed on the slab. The faint light washed upward, painting his face in shifting patterns. The disc inside his chest responded to the stone with small, steady pulses, like two hearts learning to keep time together.

He felt the weight of what they had done pressing down on him.

They had turned why into something visible.

The universe would not let that stand without asking for proof.

He had just begun to form that thought when the air changed.

It did not move. It did not chill or warm. It condensed. The space between breaths felt as if it had suddenly acquired density. Conversations faltered. Heads turned.

The Advocate appeared without approach or arrival.

It was simply present.

One moment the hall was full of humans and their fragile reasons. The next, there was a presence among them that did not occupy space in the way bodies did. It was both within the room and around it, as if the hall had been swallowed by its attention.

Some of the Reckoning inhaled sharply. Others froze in place. No one screamed. The Advocate did not provoke terror. It provoked awareness.

Ardent felt the disc in his chest stir, not in alarm, but in recognition, as if something inside him acknowledged an older relative.

He stepped forward.

"You are changing the shape of humanity," the Advocate said.

The voice did not echo. It did not need air. It existed in the same place the Why Engine existed, in the layer where intention met structure.

"Purpose bends existence," the Advocate continued. "Existence does not bend without cost."

The Reckoning shifted uneasily. Several of them looked at Ardent, not for guidance, but for translation.

Ardent narrowed his eyes.

"We know purpose is not free," he said. "We are willing to pay for it."

The Advocate tilted its head in a gesture that suggested curiosity, though its form gave nothing away.

"You misunderstand," it said. "You do not select the price. The price arises naturally from what you value. If you attempt to choose a different cost, you are no longer paying for meaning. You are paying for comfort."

Ardent took another step closer.

"Then tell me what it is," he said. "Tell me what we must give."

The Advocate did not answer immediately. The pause did not feel like hesitation. It felt like a calculation reaching completion.

When it spoke again, its words guarded the boundary between revelation and sentence.

"Meaning demands sacrifice," it said. "Not belief. Not energy. Not obedience. Meaning requires something that cannot be replaced. Something that anchors your existence within reality."

Ardent clenched his fists at his sides.

"We have already risked survival," he said. "We have challenged the Exchange. We have turned against the Bureau. We have allowed the Contest to begin. Is that not enough?"

The Advocate shook its head.

"Survival is circumstance," it replied. "Circumstance proves nothing. Purpose requires loss. Only a wound proves that a choice touched reality."

The phrase settled over the hall like a fine dust. People did not immediately grasp its full implication, but they felt its weight.

Ardent felt a cold pressure gather behind his ribs.

"What kind of wound?" he asked quietly.

The Advocate regarded him with something that might have been mistaken for pity if it had belonged to a human face.

"You must give up what anchors you," it said. "Something you love. Something you trust. Something that holds your why in place."

Ardent's breath caught.

Images moved through his mind in a rapid, chaotic sequence.

Merca Lin on the bench, eyes clear and hollow, speaking calmly about the absence of desire.

Joran dropping to his knees under Directive Two, his purpose leaking out of him until only function remained.

The Unburdened, swaying gently as they whispered about peace without caring.

The night with Seren, the single moment in his life when wanting had felt like a truth instead of a liability.

He realized that all of those images shared one common thread.

Attachment.

Ardent's voice came out as a whisper.

"You want me to choose someone."

A few nearby members of the Reckoning flinched.

The Advocate answered with the stillness of a concept that had no interest in cruelty, only precision.

"No," it said. "The universe does not want a selected victim. The universe wants proof. Meaning cannot stay in the realm of talk. It must change reality. It must break something that cannot be restored."

Ardent turned away from the Advocate, unable to hold its formless gaze. He looked at the people in the hall.

Sera, who had cried through her first statement of purpose, terrified that she would die without creating anything that mattered.

Liren, who had nearly given himself to the Unburdened and now stood near the back, still uncertain, yet tethered to a fragile reason to care again.

The older woman who rarely spoke, but always watched with fierce, protective eyes.

They were not abstractions.

They were lives that had dared to believe once more.

He closed his eyes.

"This is cruel," he said.

"It is necessary," the Advocate replied. "Without cost, purpose is decoration. Without sacrifice, belief is performance. Without wounds, meaning is pretend."

A trembling silence filled the hall. Some of the Reckoning lowered their heads. Others remained rigid, as if refusing to show that the words had struck them.

Ardent shook his head.

"We can show meaning without destroying someone," he insisted.

The Advocate's voice softened slightly.

"Then why has humanity never done it before?"

The question pierced Ardent in a place older than logic. Memories rose from depths he had not visited in years.

He saw himself as a boy asking his instructor why the system existed instead of how it worked. He heard her say that why led nowhere. He remembered the quiet fear in her eyes, the unspoken warning that purpose was dangerous.

He saw civilizations in the Forbidden Collections that had torn themselves apart over divine reasons and ideological destinies they believed were absolute and unquestionable.

He saw the Council of Survival choosing the Exchange, not out of ignorance, but out of terror that uncontrolled meaning would finish what extinction had begun.

Every time humanity had claimed a why with full passion, it had also produced someone who suffered for it.

Perhaps the Advocate was not imposing a new rule.

Perhaps it was naming an old one.

Ardent opened his eyes with anger burning behind them.

The Advocate was no longer standing in front of him.

It was at his back.

Its presence pressed inward, not heavy, but inescapable, like the feeling that a decision was already waiting and he was only catching up to it.

"You created the Reckoning," it said. "You awakened questions that had been sleeping. You challenged the Exchange. You drew attention from Kolinar. You altered the axis of your species."

Its voice dropped slightly.

"Now the universe wants to know if you can carry what you have pulled down."

Ardent swallowed.

"What if I refuse?" he asked.

"Then humanity will continue without purpose," the Advocate said. "No one will suffer from wanting what they cannot have. No one will fight over reasons. No one will die for an idea. You will eat and work and age. You will rest without expectation. You will be content without caring."

It paused.

"The Unburdened are the beginning of that future. Harmony without direction. Comfort without identity."

Ardent saw them again in his memory. Their soft smiles. Their calm eyes. Their gentle dismissal of effort.

It did not look like doom.

It looked like the end of struggle.

The Advocate continued.

"There are fates worse than death," it said. "You have already seen one sitting by the fountain."

Ardent flinched.

He did not need the name.

Merca.

He remembered her voice.

This does not hurt. Everything is quiet. Everything is fine.

He felt the wound reopen.

Fine was the most frightening word he had ever heard.

He turned back to the Advocate, jaw tight.

"If meaning requires sacrifice, show me who must be sacrificed."

The Advocate regarded him without judgment.

"You have misunderstood again," it said. "Meaning is not taken out of someone. Meaning must be given by someone. The cost is not destruction from the outside. The cost is willingness from within. There is no proof of purpose without a voluntary loss."

Ardent's voice dropped to a rasp.

"So someone must choose to surrender something that defines them."

"Yes," the Advocate said. "With full awareness. Without coercion. Without the comfort of believing they will receive it back."

The chill that moved through Ardent then had nothing to do with fear of pain. It had everything to do with the recognition of fairness.

This was not a demand for punishment.

It was a demand for honesty.

Someone had to give up their why in order to prove that the rest of humanity's why was not a painted surface.

Ardent looked at the hall again.

Faces turned toward him with trust, confusion, and a quiet hope that he could pull them through whatever was coming.

Somewhere inside, a voice that sounded uncomfortably like his own said,

If you truly believe what you say, then the cost must fall on you.

His mind recoiled.

He thought of Seren suddenly, without choosing to. Her face in the flickering light of Edelon. Her voice cracking when she had asked if purpose was worth annihilation. The moment her hand trembled against his skin, holding on to something she did not trust herself to want.

She had believed then.

Now she stood on the other side of the Contest, convinced that removal of meaning was mercy.

There was no simple villain here.

Not the Bureau.

Not Kolinar.

Not even the Exchange.

Only different answers to the same unbearable question.

How much is purpose worth?

Ardent forced himself back into the present.

"Someone must give up their why," he said, to make sure he had heard correctly.

The Advocate nodded once.

"Only then," it said, "will the universe believe that the rest of yours is real."

The Reckoning began to murmur, the sound edging into panic. The hall suddenly felt smaller.

Ardent looked directly at the Advocate.

"Who?" he asked.

The Advocate did not offer names. It never did.

"You already know who," it answered.

Ardent closed his eyes.

He did know.

Not because the Advocate had placed the thought in his mind, but because his own conscience had walked ahead of him and waited with its hands folded, patient and unforgiving.

Meaning does not live in theories.

Meaning lives in what you are willing to lose.

The Advocate's presence faded until it became indistinguishable from the air. One final sentence remained, not heard but understood.

A purpose that costs nothing is worth nothing.

The hall felt louder after it vanished, even though no one had raised their voice.

Ardent stood very still.

He could feel every set of eyes on him. Some full of questions. Some flashing with fear. Some quietly pleading for him to say that the Advocate had exaggerated, or that they had misunderstood, or that there would be another way.

He did not speak.

If he lied now, everything they had built would rot from the inside.

He stepped back from the slab, pinching the bridge of his nose, trying to steady his breathing.

Behind him, the conversations began to sharpen.

"What did it say?"

"Did you hear? Someone has to give something up."

"Give what?"

"Who?"

Merca sat on a cushion in the corner, hands folded calmly in her lap. She watched the agitation without any internal disturbance. Her eyes took in the scene, but nothing within her moved in response.

She was the shape of what awaited them if they failed.

Ardent forced himself to walk back toward the group.

He could not tell them everything.

Not yet.

But he could not hide the truth entirely either.

They parted for him as he approached, creating a hollow ring around him and the slab.

He spoke without raising his voice.

"The Advocate has confirmed what we already knew in fragments," he said. "Meaning is not theoretical. It must draw blood. The universe will not believe a purpose that does not alter reality in a way that cannot be undone."

He let that sink in.

"It is not asking for a sacrifice chosen by committee. It is not asking for a victim. It is asking for someone who will voluntarily surrender something that defines them."

Sera's face went pale.

"Someone has to die," she whispered.

Ardent shook his head.

"No. Death is not the only cost. Death is the absence of experience. Meaning requires the loss of something inside experience."

He searched for words.

"Imagine living without the one reason that holds you upright," he said quietly. "Imagine continuing on, aware of what you once had, and knowing that you will never have it again, because you gave it up so that the rest of us could keep ours."

The room shuddered.

Liren swallowed hard.

"Who would do that?" he asked.

Ardent did not answer.

Not out loud.

His mind was quiet for a moment.

Then, slowly, reality aligned around the only truthful possibility.

If he asked this of someone else, he would become everything he claimed to stand against.

If he demanded it, the act would stop being purpose and become coercion.

If he selected a candidate, he would turn a volunteer into a sacrifice.

There was only one person he had the right to offer.

Himself.

The realization did not come as drama. It came as acceptance. It felt like setting down a secret he had been carrying for years.

He did not speak it yet.

The disc in his chest pulsed hard enough to make him catch his breath.

The slab's symbols shifted in a corner of the stone, as if reacting to an unspoken decision.

Ardent pressed his palm against it to steady the pattern.

"We are not there yet," he said. "We still have time within the cycle. We still have reasons to strengthen. We still have lives to touch. When the moment of cost arrives, it will be clear. It must be."

The woman with bright eyes stared at him, suspicion and concern mingling.

"You are holding something back," she said softly.

He met her gaze.

"I am holding back a conclusion that is not ready," he replied. "If I state it now, it becomes destiny instead of choice."

She studied him for a moment, then nodded once, more from respect than agreement.

The murmur in the hall slowly receded. People settled back into small groups again, but this time their conversations were sharper, more raw.

They did not speak about theories now.

They spoke about what each of them would be willing to lose.

A relationship.

A memory.

A talent.

A dream.

An entire sense of self.

Meaning had become personal in a way it had never been before.

Ardent listened to the fragments.

"I would give up my work."

"I would give up my art."

"I would give up my name."

"I would give up my fear."

He knew that most of them did not yet understand the depth of what the Advocate had described. It was easy to offer something in imagination when the world still felt the same.

He also knew that somewhere among them, someone else might be forming the same conclusion he had.

Perhaps he would not be the only one willing to bear the cost.

Perhaps that would make his choice heavier, not lighter.

He looked once more at Merca.

She sat with perfect composure, watching the fountain of human effort surge and recede around her.

Her why had been taken.

Now someone else would have to give theirs.

Not taken.

Given.

Ardent turned back to the slab. The patterns flickered at his touch, then steadied.

The Why Engine was still building.

He understood something severe and beautiful as he watched it.

The universe did not hate meaning.

The universe wanted to see whether meaning was strong enough to stand when it hurt the one who carried it.

He placed his hand over his heart.

The disc pulsed in answer.

He whispered so quietly that no one but the stone and the unseen listener could hear him.

"If blood is required," he said, "let it be mine."

The slab trembled almost imperceptibly.

The air felt colder, not from temperature, but from the knowledge that a path had quietly formed ahead of them.

Around him, the Reckoning continued to speak, continued to doubt, continued to choose.

They did not know yet that innocence had ended.

They only knew that they wanted to believe.

Ardent stood in the middle of their fragile faith and understood the terrible truth.

To prove that humanity deserved meaning, something precious would have to be relinquished.

Not symbolically.

Not in metaphor.

Finally and forever.

CHAPTER TWENTY-THREE:

A REASON THAT BLEEDS

The night over District Seven felt thinner than before.

It was not colder. The stars did not vanish. The city lights still glowed in their careful, regulated grids. Yet the air held an absence that had no name. It felt as if something essential had already been taken from the world and the atmosphere had not yet learned how to settle around the missing piece.

Inside the Reckoning hall, the slab pulsed with soft light. Lines and symbols flowed across its surface like a living script, mapping reasons that had been spoken and decisions that had been made. The glow had the rhythm of a slow heartbeat, as if the stone was breathing along with the people gathered around it.

Small clusters of Reckoning members spoke in low voices. They did not talk about logistics. They did not talk about schedules or contingencies. They spoke about what they would miss if meaning disappeared. They spoke about childhood moments when they had first felt that life might matter. They spoke about the terror of discovering that those moments were not guaranteed.

For the first time, many of them spoke not as witnesses to a movement, but as participants in a risk that could touch their own lives.

Ardent Voss stood apart, near the edge of the hall where the light from the slab began to fade into shadow.

His thoughts were sharp and heavy.

The Advocate's words circled him, closing tighter with every repetition in his mind.

Meaning demands sacrifice.

Something irreplaceable.

Something loved.

Something that anchors your why.

He had spent years inside the Bureau unearthing hidden patterns, uncovering concealed structures, exposing the lies that institutions told themselves. He had learned to treat truth as a distant object to be examined, measured, and recorded.

Now truth had moved. It was no longer an object.

It was walking toward him.

He looked toward the entrance.

The doors opened.

Merca Lin walked in.

She moved with the unhurried pace of someone who felt no urgency. Not slow from fatigue, not weak from grief, simply unbound from intention. Her steps were precise, but lacked direction. Her hands rested calmly at her sides. Her shoulders were relaxed, her breathing steady.

Her eyes were clear.

They were not bright with purpose.

They were not dull with despair.

They were calm in a way that felt profoundly wrong.

She was the quiet blueprint of what the Bureau wanted humanity to become.

A life without why.

Conversations in the hall faltered, then faded. Heads turned. Some people looked relieved to see her, thinking of the Merca who had once greeted new arrivals and helped them find words for their reasons. Others looked afraid, remembering the last time they saw her on a bench by a fountain, at peace in a way that looked more like erasure than healing.

Ardent stepped away from the wall.

Every step he took toward her weighed more than the last.

He stopped in front of her.

"Merca," he said, "do you remember me?"

Her gaze focused on his face. Recognition passed through her expression, perfectly intact.

"Yes," she said. "I know who you are."

Her tone was polite. There was no warmth, no reluctance. Recognition without reaction.

Ardent swallowed.

"Do you remember what you believed?" he asked.

Merca looked past him for a moment, toward the slab, then back.

"I remember believing," she said after a pause. "I do not remember why I cared."

Her answer was not bitter.

It was simply accurate.

The words slipped into the hall like a blade wrapped in silk.

Behind Ardent, someone exhaled sharply. Another person covered their mouth. The Reckoning had seen her absence before, but hearing it named so calmly made it real in a new way.

Ardent's chest tightened.

"I cannot accept a world where this is your fate," he said.

Merca tilted her head, considering his statement with distant curiosity.

"It does not hurt," she replied. "There is no fear. No urgency. No weight."

She spoke the words some part of humanity had always wanted to hear.

No fear. No urgency. No weight.

Ardent shook his head.

"That is the problem," he said softly. "Pain means there was something worth protecting. Fear means there was something that could be lost. You deserve a reason for your existence. You deserve to feel that you matter."

Merca blinked.

"What does deserve mean," she asked, "when nothing matters?"

The Reckoning shuddered as if the entire room had flinched.

Her question was not philosophical.

It was a doorway opening into perfect oblivion.

Ardent took a step closer. He could see the faint lines at the corners of her eyes, the marks of a person who had once laughed and once worried and once tried. Those lines remained. The story that had carved them did not.

"I am going to give you something," he said.

Her brows drew together slightly, not in concern, but in confusion.

"Why?" she asked.

She did not ask from suspicion.

She asked because motives were now irrelevant to her. Action was separated from consequence. Cause was separated from effect.

Ardent's hand moved automatically to his chest.

He felt the disc pulse beneath his palm, alive and alert, as if it sensed the direction of his thought and recoiled.

"Because," he said, "you were the first person who made me believe this was possible."

Images rose in his mind.

Merca's face the day he first entered the hall. The way her eyes had lit when he described Edelon. The tremor in her voice when she had said that purpose felt like a room she had not known she was allowed to enter. The moment she had pressed her hand against the cold stone of the unfinished slab and whispered her reason, and the stone had answered with its first fragile spark of light.

"You helped me find my why," he said. "You helped me see what humanity was losing. You were the first to prove that we want meaning, even when we are afraid of it. You were the spark that made the Reckoning real."

His hand pressed harder against his chest.

"And I cannot let the universe erase the one who ignited us."

The disc pulsed violently now. Pain shot through his ribs, sharp and electric. It felt like resistance. Or warning. Or grief.

Several members of the Reckoning stepped forward.

The woman with bright eyes spoke first, her voice tight.

"Ardent," she said, "you know what the Advocate told you. If you give up what anchors you, you will lose your direction. You will lose the reason that holds you together."

He nodded without looking away from Merca.

"Yes," he said. "I know."

Another voice joined, shaking.

"You cannot lead us without purpose," a young man said. "We need you. You are the one the Exchange talks to. You are the one Kolinar fears. You are the one who carries the disc. If you lose your why, the Reckoning will lose its center."

Ardent turned slightly to face them.

"I am not giving up leadership," he said. "I am giving up the origin of my why. The first spark. The personal reason that made me start. Meaning must outgrow me, or it is only an extension of my story. If all of this collapses when I fall, then it was never humanity's meaning. It was only mine."

Gasps spread through the hall like a small, sudden storm.

Some stepped backward.

Some stepped closer.

The woman with bright eyes shook her head, tears gathering.

"Why you?" she whispered. "Why not someone else?"

Ardent smiled sadly.

"Because I am the one who cannot ask it of anyone else," he said. "If I am willing to ask another person to carry this wound, then everything I have said about purpose becomes another form of control."

His voice steadied, iron at the core.

"If the universe demands that someone bleed, then the one who called for the Reckoning should step forward first."

Silence settled again.

The slab's light dimmed, as if bracing.

He turned back to Merca.

"I give you my why," he said.

For a heartbeat, nothing happened.

Then the slab erupted.

Light burst outward from its surface in a surge that flooded the hall. Symbols broke apart, separating into fragments that spun through the air like shards of luminous glass. The entire room shook, not physically, but conceptually. The world felt as if it had taken a step sideways.

Ardent felt the disc seize inside his chest.

A force pulled at him from within, not dragging, not tearing, but demanding release. He sank to one knee, teeth clenched, breath ragged.

The Reckoning cried out.

Merca stared, eyes widening as she watched the man in front of her become the center of a storm she could not interpret.

A line of light formed between Ardent and the slab.

Then another formed between Ardent and Merca.

The two lines met at his chest.

The disc flared.

A beam of light, narrow and impossibly bright, shot from his body into hers. It was not fire. It was not energy as the Bureau understood it. It was the transfer of orientation, the handing over of a place in reality that had once belonged to him alone.

Ardent's vision blurred into white and shadow. He heard the sound of people calling his name as if from underwater.

For an instant, he felt everything.

Every reason he had ever held. Every moment when he had chosen meaning over safety, questioning over compliance, hope over surrender. Every memory of standing in Edelon and feeling the horror of a species that had survived by amputating its soul.

He felt all of it.

Then he felt it letting go.

The beam drove into Merca's chest.

Her body jerked. Her eyes flew open wider than before. Inside them, for a brief, staggering moment, a storm danced. Flickers of memory, shards of fear, sparks of wonder. The echo of every question she had ever asked, every doubt she had ever hidden, every hope she had once dared to hold and then forgotten.

Her hand flew to her chest, fingers clawing at empty air as if an invisible weight had just landed there.

"I remember wanting something," she whispered.

Her voice trembled.

The storm in her eyes steadied.

"I remember wanting to know why I was here."

Tears welled and spilled over her cheeks.

Not from pain.

From return.

The Reckoning watched in a silence deeper than any they had ever known. They did not shift. They did not breathe loudly. They barely seemed alive themselves.

Something sacred was occurring in front of them.

Merca lifted her gaze to the slab.

The stone responded.

New symbols erupted across its surface, connecting to older lines, reweaving broken paths. The map of purpose shifted, expanding to include a point that had once been dark and was now brightly alive.

She turned to Ardent.

"You gave this to me," she said.

Her voice no longer floated without anchor.

It struck reality and stayed there.

Ardent swayed.

His legs felt hollow.

His vision doubled, then steadied, then dimmed again.

The slab's glow altered. There was a subtle withdrawal, a quiet recognition that the source of one of its original threads had moved.

Merca stepped closer and placed her hand over his where it rested on his chest.

"My reason is clear now," she said. "Humanity exists to create meaning that did not exist before. Not to receive it. Not to inherit it. Not to borrow it. To make it. Even when the making hurts. Especially when it hurts."

Ardent managed a weak smile.

"Good," he whispered. "Then it is yours now. Truly yours."

She squeezed his hand.

"What is your reason now?" she asked.

He opened his mouth.

No answer came.

His smile faded.

He looked at her, at the slab, at the people around him.

He felt their gazes, their fears, their hopes.

He understood every concept.

He remembered every argument.

He could recite the principles of the Reckoning as clearly as ever.

But there was nothing inside those understandings that pulled him forward.

No tug.

No urge.

No direction.

"I do not know," he said.

The hall froze.

The words echoed through the chamber, emptier than any silence.

Ardent Voss stood upright, fully conscious, memory intact, intellect sharp, awareness functioning.

And empty of direction.

He had not lost identity. He knew his own name. He knew his history. He remembered Edelon. He remembered Seren. He remembered the moment he had touched the Disc of Origin and felt humanity's first purpose awaken inside him.

He believed none of it on a level that mattered.

It was all accurate.

It was no longer his reason.

Terror rippled through the Reckoning.

Someone whispered, "We have broken him."

Another answered, voice shaking, "No. He chose this."

A third could not speak at all. Their mouth moved around unfinished words.

Ardent reached for the slab with a trembling hand.

The stone remained warm beneath his fingers.

The symbols did not brighten at his touch.

They no longer recognized him as one who held purpose.

To the Why Engine, he was now a witness, not a source.

A man who knew too much and no longer knew why it mattered.

Merca stepped back, her eyes burning with a light that was too intense to be simple gratitude. She seemed larger somehow, not in stature, but in presence. Her posture carried the weight of someone who had just been handed a responsibility that extended far beyond her life.

She turned toward the hall.

"Meaning is not given," she said, voice clear and unwavering. "Meaning is chosen. It can be shared. It can be protected. It can be fought for. It can be lost."

She looked again at Ardent.

"And it can be given at a cost."

The hall erupted.

Not in chaos.

In sound that carried grief and awe in equal measure.

Some shouted cries of disbelief.

Some wept openly, hands covering their faces.

Some sank to their knees, not in worship, but in shock that a person they trusted had willingly become the proof they had needed.

Others stood rigid, fists clenched, anger rising at a universe that would demand such a thing.

Purpose, once fragile and theoretical, was now undeniable.

It had drawn blood.

Ardent stood in the center of the reaction.

He did not flinch.

He did not step away.

He watched them all with calm, distant eyes.

He understood that they were changed.

He did not feel responsible for that change.

He did not feel anything about it at all.

The absence was not numbness.

Numbness suggests that sensation is blocked.

This was absence of the source that gives sensation meaning.

The difference was subtle and terrible.

The woman with bright eyes approached him slowly, as if moving toward someone who had been injured in a way she did not understand.

"Do you regret it?" she asked.

Ardent considered the question.

He could weigh the concept of regret. He could list arguments for and against. He could predict the effects of regret on his future choices.

He could not feel regret itself.

"I understand that I might have," he said carefully. "Before."

She closed her eyes for a moment, then opened them and nodded, even as tears slid down her cheeks.

"Then it was real," she whispered. "Your purpose was real."

Merca faced the group.

Her voice rose.

"Listen to me," she said. "The universe has accused us of playing with meaning. Of treating purpose like a toy, like a story we tell ourselves to feel better. It has demanded proof that we are not pretending."

She pointed at Ardent.

"That proof stands in front of you. He gave up the reason that anchored him. Not because a god required it. Not because a ruler ordered it. Because he believed that our why was worth more than his own."

She lifted her hand toward the slab.

"I will not let that gift collapse into memory. My why is clear. Humanity exists to create meaning that did not exist before. I will carry that meaning now. I will speak it. I will build with it. I will bleed for it."

The slab shone brighter than ever.

Symbols cascaded into place, forming arcs that curved around Merca like the outline of a new constellation.

The Reckoning raised their heads.

Some repeated her words.

Some found others.

"I will fight for our why."

"I will not let his loss be pointless."

"I will not retreat to quiet."

"I will not choose to stop caring."

The air in the hall vibrated with aligned intention.

For the first time, the Why Engine produced not only light, but pressure. The sense of a field expanding outward, pushing against the fabric of whatever watched them.

Far above, beyond sight, something in the Exchange's endless ledger shivered. A value that had always been theoretical gained a marker labeled proven. Kolinar, in its distant domain, felt the disturbance of a species that had paid a personal cost for manufactured purpose and did not fall apart.

The Advocate watched.

It did not intervene.

It did not congratulate.

It recorded.

It bore witness to the fact that humanity had finally stopped speaking about meaning as if it were a philosophy and had started treating it as a reality that could hurt.

In the center of the hall, Ardent Voss stood very still.

He listened to the voices. He comprehended every word. He understood that he had become the wound that proved meaning was real.

He understood that the Reckoning would now move without him at its core.

He understood that the story had changed.

He did not feel pride.

He did not feel loss.

He simply existed, aware, intelligent, and detached from the one thing that had once made existence bearable.

Merca turned back to him, eyes shining with purpose and sorrow.

"You are not empty," she said gently. "You are the place where our meaning cut into reality. The hole proves the blade."

He studied her expression, recognizing the compassion in it without being moved by it.

"I am glad," he said, "that it is enough for you."

She nodded.

"It is enough for me," she replied. "Now we must make sure it is enough for the universe."

The Reckoning gathered closer to her, drawn by the gravity of someone who now carried a why that had cost blood.

Ardent watched them form around her.

The center had shifted.

The Reckoning had not been defined by what they gained.

They had been defined by what they lost.

And somewhere far beyond the sky of Halo, the Contest altered its tone.

Humanity had shown that its reasons were not decorations.

They were capable of bleeding.

The universe had taken notice.

CHAPTER TWENTY-FOUR

THE SILENCE BEFORE WHY

The world did not end with thunder. No armies appeared at the horizon. The sky did not break open in fire or judgment. There were no great explosions announced by news feeds or collapsing towers of civilization. None of the endings humanity used to imagine ever arrived.

The end of Book One began with quiet.

A quiet so complete it felt intentional. A quiet that did not wait for permission. A quiet that descended like something alive.

The Reckoning hall glowed softly. The slab pulsed with symbols that formed and reformed like constellations trying to remember their own shape. Every thread of light on its surface represented a reason spoken by someone who refused to stop caring. Each reason sparked against the next, generating a map of purpose no one had ever known how to draw before.

This was not decoration. This was evidence.

Merca Lin stood before the slab. Her breath was steady. Her hands did not shake. Her presence was calm, yet nothing about her felt passive. There was motion in her stillness, like a bowstring drawn back and waiting to be released. Purpose lived in her now, not as a thought, but as a pulse.

Ardent Voss stood behind her.

He did not sway. His gaze was not empty. His posture was not weakened. Nothing about him seemed broken except the single thing that defined him. His mind held clarity. His memory held precision. He remembered who he had been, what he had believed, and the world he had helped awaken.

He simply no longer had a reason of his own.

He had become the cost that proved meaning was not invention but sacrifice.

People who had once looked to him for direction now watched him as someone who bore witness. He was no longer the one who moved the Reckoning forward. He was the one who stood where purpose had left a scar.

Merca glanced at him once, searching for the fire that had once burned in his eyes. When she found only reflection, her expression shifted. Not toward sorrow. Toward resolve. Someone had to carry meaning now. The universe had taken its price, and someone had to answer with action.

The Reckoning did not wait for Ardent to lead.

They waited for him to watch.

THE SKY ANSWERS

Light rippled across the sky like ink spreading through water. People lifted their heads in every district of Halo. Children froze mid stride. The Unburdened paused mid breath. Bureau agents stopped mid sentence. The city became still enough that heartbeat and thought felt louder than sound.

The sky did not tear open.

It recognized the moment.

A single line appeared overhead, not spoken by any voice, not projected by screens, yet understood instantly by every mind:

HUMANITY HAS SPOKEN

The slab's symbols surged in brightness. Merca stepped forward. She did not gesture. She did not raise her voice. Her intention was enough. The air adjusted around her, as if meaning was gravity and she had become its center.

She spoke.

"Humanity exists to create meaning where none was given. We refuse a universe without why. We choose struggle over emptiness. We choose consequence over silence. We choose to matter."

The words did not echo.

They entered the world.

Each syllable rose like sparks drawn into currents beyond sight. The slab answered, its symbols flaring, ripping into new patterns. What had been fragments began to align. A structure formed.

Not a statement.

A direction.

The voice of the Exchange responded.

It did not shout. It did not roar. It altered the world by speaking into the architecture of belief.

"MEANING WITHOUT TEST IS FABLE. PURPOSE WITHOUT TRIAL IS NOISE. HUMANITY HAS DECLARED REASON. HUMANITY WILL PROVE REASON."

A new line formed beneath:

THE AUDIT IS CANCELLED

Gasps filled the plaza. Hope, raw and uncontrollable, surged like lightning through every person who heard it.

Then the sky continued:

THE CONTEST BEGINS

The hope collapsed into something sharper. Something that tasted like both invitation and danger.

The air thickened. It felt as though the world had taken a breath and forgotten how to release it.

Kolinar appeared beside the words, a silhouette carved from starlight.

"Humanity has trespassed into origin. Meaning cannot exist without anchor. Present your cause to the universe and defend it. Creation demands confrontation."

The Advocate's voice followed, softer and infinitely heavier.

"Humanity has chosen to matter. Now humanity will be measured by what that choice changes."

The sky flickered, and a final proclamation appeared. It was not a warning. It was not a comfort.

It was the threshold.

THE NEXT QUESTION DECIDES YOUR SPECIES

Then everything went still.

The clouds. The plaza. The Reckoning. Even the city seemed to lock in place, as if sound itself had been removed from possibility.

Silence fell like a gate.

THE RECKONING BREATHES

Merca stepped away from the slab. Her face held no triumph. She carried no signs of victory. She was something more unsettling.

She was aligned.

People looked at her not as a leader, but as a mirror in which they saw themselves transformed. For the first time in perhaps the entire history of the species, humanity had someone who did not demand belief, but embodied it.

Ardent stepped forward.

The room's focus shifted instinctively, out of habit, out of memory, out of the echo of the man he used to be.

He blinked once. His voice came quietly, as if spoken from a vast interior distance.

"I remember who I was," he said. "I remember why I cared. I remember every reason spoken in this hall. I can explain purpose. I can teach it. I can see it in others."

He paused.

"But I do not feel it. I cannot find my reason. I lost the origin of my why. That was the price."

The words hurt far more than any scream.

Some members of the Reckoning bowed their heads. Some pressed their hands over their hearts. Some whispered prayers to gods who may never have existed until this moment. Others stared at Ardent as if watching a man who had crossed a river no one else knew how to survive.

Merca placed her hand on his shoulder.

"You gave me your reason," she said. "Now I will act on it."

He nodded. No emotion crossed his face.

"You were the beginning," she added. "You do not have to be the end."

Ardent's eyes shifted, not with feeling, but with comprehension.

"I am the question now," he said.

"Yes," she replied. "And we are the answer."

THE FINAL MOMENT

Light rippled across the city again.

This time it was not text.

It was a symbol.

It did not resemble any human design. It was not geometric. It was not organic. It looked like something between map and wound, between possibility and consequence. It hovered in the air above the district.

Every mind recognized what it represented without knowing how.

The next phase.

The next trial.

The next reckoning.

The symbol pulsed once. The slab answered with a soft tremor. The lights of the district flickered. The symbol pulsed again. The sky darkened, not into night, but into something that waited.

The world did not feel threatened.

The world felt watched.

The people of the Reckoning looked back at Ardent Voss.

He did not tremble.

He did not smile.

He did not break.

He asked the only question that could still be asked in a world that had run out of answers.

"Why now?"

The sky did not respond with sound.

It responded with silence.

The silence did not comfort.

It opened.

Like a doorway.

Like a threshold.

Like the breath before a universe decides whether you belong in it.

Humanity was no longer being audited.

Humanity had been invited to prove it deserved existence.

The Contest of Meaning had begun.

The silence waited for the next reason.

The next sacrifice.

The next voice.

BOOK TWO

THE CONTEST OF MEANING

COMING SOON

Don't miss out!

Visit the website below and you can sign up to receive emails whenever Ilir Nina publishes a new book. There's no charge and no obligation.

https://books2read.com/r/B-A-SAREF-CBLYI

BOOKS 2 READ

Connecting independent readers to independent writers.

Did you love *The Ledger of Worlds*? Then you should read *My Flight to Freedom*[1] by Ilir Nina!

[2]

My Flight to Freedom is a memoir of escape, survival, and becoming.

Born under an oppressive system, Ilir Nina grew up where choices were limited and silence was a form of safety. Leaving meant risking everything, yet staying meant losing himself. What follows is not a simple story of immigration, but a deeper reckoning with identity, addiction, ambition, and the quiet cost of reinvention.

---

1. https://books2read.com/u/mvlkpX

2. https://books2read.com/u/mvlkpX

From dislocation and early survival to professional success and personal collapse, this memoir traces the long arc of freedom not as a destination, but as a discipline. Success brings comfort, but not clarity. Numbers provide order, but not meaning. Recovery demands honesty where achievement once hid the truth.

Written with restraint and reflection, *My Flight to Freedom* explores what it means to build a life in a new country while carrying the weight of the old one. It is a story about leaving, arriving, falling apart, and learning that freedom is not something granted by borders, but something earned through self examination.

This book is for readers drawn to memoirs of resilience, recovery, and the difficult work of becoming fully human.

Read more at https://ilirninaauthor.com/.

Also by Ilir Nina

my flight to freedom series
Echoes of the Mind
The Final Audit
My flight to freedom II: Shadows and Light: Survival and the American Dream

The Ledger of Worlds
The Ledger of Worlds

Standalone
My Flight to Freedom

Watch for more at https://ilirninaauthor.com/.

About the Author

About the Author

Ilir Nina, CPA, EA, MSAT, is a Certified Public Accountant, Enrolled Agent, entrepreneur, and author with more than three decades of experience helping individuals, families, and businesses navigate some of life's most challenging financial moments.

Born in Albania and later immigrating to the United States, Ilir built his career through perseverance, education, and a commitment to helping others. Over the years, he has worked with thousands of clients facing audits, tax disputes, business challenges, financial hardship, and personal crossroads. Through those experiences, he discovered that behind every tax return is a human story and behind every financial decision is a life being lived.

A recovering alcoholic with more than twenty-eight years of sobriety, Ilir brings a unique perspective shaped by resilience, gratitude, and second chances. His writing explores the intersection of success, purpose, personal growth, and the lessons that often emerge from adversity.

He is the owner of Idaho Tax & Bookkeeping Services, LLC, and lives in Eagle, Idaho, with his wife, Anile, a licensed professional counselor. Together they have dedicated their lives to helping others find clarity, healing, and hope.

The Final Audit: What Matters When the Numbers Don't Add Up is a reflection on the people, experiences, and life lessons that taught him that the most important things can never be measured by numbers alone.

Read more at https://ilirninaauthor.com.

www.ingramcontent.com/pod-product-compliance
Lightning Source LLC
La Vergne TN
LVHW100514110826
845146LV00002B/632